# TEMPTING THE NEW BOSS

*a Sleeping with the Enemy novel*

# ANGELA CLAIRE

Entangled Publishing, LLC
2614 South Timberline Road
Suite 109
Fort Collins, CO 80525
Visit our website at www.entangledpublishing.com.

Brazen is an imprint of Entangled Publishing, LLC. For more information on our titles, visit www.brazenbooks.com.

Edited by Marie Loggia-Kee
Cover design by Heather Howland
Cover art from Period Images

Manufactured in the United States of America

First Edition October 2015

ENTANGLED
BRAZEN

*To the real Joey, who I love very much*

# Chapter One

"It's polite to shake a new employee's hand when it's extended." Mason Talbot's administrative assistant interrupted his reading of the draft Annual Report.

A woman stood next to Marcia. She was a little younger than him, late twenties maybe, and sported a wide, over-eager smile along with the usual polished exterior of a lawyer. Navy suit. First-day-of-work string of pearls. He took the young woman's outstretched hand and obligingly shook it.

"Camilla Anderson. Nice to meet you, Mr. Talbot."

"Yeah. You, too." No magic sparks erupted between them. He didn't touch her and know she would be his future. He didn't think much of lawyers. At all. One way or the other. They were a necessary evil as far as he was concerned. He dropped her hand and turned to Marcia. "Can I have my report back now?"

He was trying to get through the legalese of the report and sign off on it by the time he left for his trip. Reading and rereading every sentence to get the general gist of it was slowing him down. He'd solved calculus equations that were less complex.

"No. You have to leave. You can read it on the plane."

"I thought I had two hours?"

"We're fitting a meeting in on the way. Greg Porter called and said it couldn't wait. No prep needed. Just introductory." She handed him his briefcase.

"What is it?"

"Project Ripper. It's moving faster than they expected."

"Oh, European component supply. Right. I care about that one."

"Which is why I put it on your schedule. Now what about the dinner next month? I have to let them know." She waved an invitation that she had been hounding him about for the last couple days.

"No. No way."

"You don't have to give a speech. Just say 'thank you' for the award and be on your way. You care about that one, too. You know you do. All the money you've spent on—"

"Forget it. Let's go, uh…"

"Camilla. Her name is Camilla"

"Where's what's-his-name? The usual one?"

"Sam got tired of you shouting at him and forgetting his name. He said he didn't go to Yale for that. He quit. Camilla here is his replacement."

The new hire played with her pearls, a twist of the single strand around her index finger, and treated him to that wide smile again. Glossy cherry lips and teeth so white they put her jewels to shame. He had a sudden vision of tilting her heart-shaped chin up and running his tongue along the gloss, savoring the fruity taste of her. Unclasping the necklace to let it drop slowly into the satiny crevice between her breasts. Fishing it out with long strokes on her bare skin along the way.

Mason shrugged into his jacket, missing the armhole twice before he finally got it on, and looked away. *Okay, that was weird. And not good.* Where the hell had that come from? He had never looked at a *suit*—his term for one of the troop of business executives who kept his company humming—with *that* in mind, no matter how attractive she was. Suits were for advancing more important *business* agendas.

He strode out the door with the new lawyer behind him. "I hope you didn't go to Yale," he said over his shoulder.

"Harvard."

"Well, that's a little better."

"Camilla, hang back a minute," Marcia called out. "I've told the limousine to wait. You go on ahead downstairs, Mason."

S am Shreeman had tried to talk Camilla out of taking his old job, but the salary Talbot, Inc. offered spoke louder. She'd done her research on Mason Talbot before she applied for the job as his corporate counsel, and everything she saw on the record was admirable. Degree from Caltech, Ph.D. at twenty-five, CEO of his own company one short year later, and a billionaire by thirty.

"Forget the record," Shreeman had advised, "the man is practically Asperger-Syndrome-worthy."

And this from the guy who was interviewing her for the

job. Even if her predecessor's unflattering portrait of Talbot wasn't sour grapes, all she needed to do was manage to last one measly year. Then she could pay off her student loans and finally be free of the worst decision she'd ever made. Going to law school.

Uncomfortable with slurs involving developmental disorders, however, she had reminded Shreeman about the generous severance package he bragged he was getting "to keep his mouth shut"—otherwise known as a non-disparagement agreement—and he admitted, "You're right. It was just a joke anyway. But man, Talbot is downright odd. Acts like he doesn't know you're in the room half the time and the other half he treats you like shit."

Was that all? She was used to being treated like shit. She'd worked as an associate at a New York meat grinder, er, law firm, before they had the gall to repay her hundred-hour working weeks by laying her off to maintain profit margins.

Talbot's matronly assistant gestured to the black leather sofa in the corner of the office, bigger than Camilla's entire studio apartment, and placed what looked like an invitation on the coffee table, before taking a seat beside her.

A large woman with a shock of gray hair trailing down her back in a thick braid, Marcia White dressed in peasant skirts that spoke to comfort in her own body after five or so decades and referred to her boss like a recalcitrant child. Camilla was already a fan.

The assistant batted the invitation around on the coffee table with one finger, and Camilla couldn't help but notice the gold embossed script against the white background. *A thank you dinner for our generous sponsor.* There was a yellow logo of a smiley face that seemed out of keeping with the otherwise elegant invitation. *Camp for Kids* it said.

"It's so nice to meet Mr. Talbot finally," Camilla offered.

"Yeah, Mason's a doll," Ms. White said. "But the thing is, he's not so good with his, ah, *social skills*. I won't get into his family, er, personal background. But let's just say he's a little awkward sometimes, with people I mean."

Camilla didn't even dare nod. Was this some kind of post-employment test?

"I have a little job for you, Camilla. Something to keep your eye on while you're doing all that legal crap."

"Of course. Is it something to do with that invitation?"

She looked down at the white square of cardboard and laughed, as if she'd forgotten she had it, then gave it a rest. "This? No, this is a cause Mason gives a load of money to and just refuses to let them thank him for it."

Marcia scooted forward. "Now you're a smart lawyer, Camilla, but there were about a hundred other smart lawyers applying for this job, and I didn't want another Shreeman, nice as the poor kid was."

"Sure."

"So when I saw your resume and did a little more fact checking on you, about your background and all, and then you came in, I could see right away you were what we needed around here."

"And what was that?"

"Somebody to teach Mason some manners."

It was about the last thing she expected the assistant to say. She laughed, starting to stand. "I'll do my best."

Marcia yanked her back down. "I'm not kidding. With that big family of yours, you got skills from the cradle Mason doesn't know the first thing about. How to get along with people. How to, well, hide a little of yourself in a crowd. Blend in."

On interview day, the assistant *had* asked a lot about Camilla's big brood of an Irish Catholic family, eight kids in all. But of course everybody asked about that when they found out. Although it had been commonplace in her neighborhood back in Detroit, in New York it was as unusual as saying she'd been raised Amish. *How did your mother remember all your names?*

"That's nice of you to say but—"

"And then with your PR training—"

"Not exactly training. It was more like a class or two in college."

"—and your psychology degree—"

"Just a minor."

"You have all the right tools to take somebody like Mason and make him, well, a little smoother when he deals with people. Like I said, sort of teach him some manners."

"I don't think I'd be very good at that."

"You'll do fine."

"What I mean to say is I'm not comfortable with it. Correcting my boss or guiding him on anything non-legal, that is. I'd rather not."

"It was in the job description. Footnote three. Check it out if you like."

She mentally called up the vague reference to *other duties as specified by etc. etc.* It was always the fine print that got you. "No need. I concede the point."

The assistant stood up. "Thanks so much, hon. I look forward to seeing how you do."

Camilla smiled, recognizing an immovable force when

she ran into one. "No problem. I'm on it."

So in addition to the Uniform Commercial Code and Securities Acts, it looked like she needed to pick up an etiquette guide for this job.

When she got back down to the limousine, apologizing profusely for the delay, the driver nodded, and Talbot, sitting across from her, barely acknowledged her presence, staring out the window at the rainy, snarled Manhattan traffic. The car pulled out, and she pretended to read her iPhone, as if she might have some important emails to scan when in fact her work email wasn't even set up yet.

Her new boss was a little quiet—actually completely silent—but after years of listening to blowhard superiors, in title if nothing else, and seven noisy siblings, quiet was a refreshing change. She decided against trying to start a conversation right off, since he seemed distracted. It gave her an opportunity to study him.

Business casual didn't begin to describe Talbot's style. Student casual was more like it. Homeless casual may have even been closer to the truth. The jacket he'd shrugged into on his way out of the office was of a muddy color that had once been tweed but was worn down to a smooth sheen, ill-fitting at that, and his shirt was a simple T-shirt with a slogan on it that she couldn't quite read. The jeans and tennis shoes completing his outfit were beaten up enough to look chic, but she doubted that was on purpose. He clearly didn't care what he looked like.

Interesting, then, that the rest of him actually looked

quite yummy. Sure, she'd been working nonstop since she passed the bar and hadn't shared her bed in almost as long as that, but she still recognized attractive when she saw it.

With his overlong curly black hair, dark blue eyes, and inky lashes, Talbot had a distinctly Byronic thing going on, with none of the eccentric or tyrannical undertones her predecessor had hinted at.

Even now, she couldn't help but notice his long fingers, nails short and blunt, as he rested them against his full lower lip, or the way his chin was slightly squared, making his angular face more than just planes and hollows. His legs, which took up most of the space between the two sides of the limo, were crossed as he leaned toward the window, completely still. What was going on in his head? She thought about his assistant's surprising last-minute addition to her work responsibilities. He didn't look the slightest bit ill at ease or awkward.

But most people didn't sit in absolute silence with a new employee. Small talk might be a nice way to ease into the gentle tutoring that she supposed she should be flattered Marcia wanted her to undertake. So she said, "Horrible weather we're having, isn't it? And it's not even April showers, right? What do October showers bring I wonder. Halloween?"

No slight turn of his head in her direction. No hum. And above all no talk, small or otherwise. It was as if he hadn't heard, glued to the sight of the bleary city streets, blaring honks punctuated by jarring starts and stops, not just for the limousine, but all the cars around them. An occasional biker veered in and out of traffic for variety, risking his life in the name of whatever package he was delivering.

"I don't know how they do that," she tried again, leaving the statement ambiguous so as to prompt the obvious response. *Who?* Or even *You mean bikers?*

But again there was nothing. Thinking of her little brother, Joey, who was hard of hearing, among his other issues, she wondered if maybe that was part of Talbot's problem. Was it possible he had some hearing loss and was hiding it behind his aloof exterior?

"I said I don't know how they do it. *Bikers*." Spoken as loudly as she would to Joey if he wasn't facing her.

That did the trick. He turned sharply toward her. "Is there some reason why you're shouting at me?"

"Oh, sorry." She forced a laugh. "I thought maybe you hadn't heard me. Just making conversation."

His phone buzzed with a text, and he glanced at it, then at her. "I thought you were my lawyer."

"I am."

"Hmmm." He pocketed his phone. "Marcia says it's going to be part of your job to make me more amenable to people and help me with my social skills."

Her mouth dropped open.

"Of which she says I don't have any."

She was starting to think maybe the assistant didn't, either.

One corner of his mouth turned up, a dimple making him look boyish. "Good luck with that," he murmured.

The limousine stopped, and the driver came around to the curb to get their door. An open umbrella was clutched in his hand, but Talbot walked right by it, long strides in the rain toward the Time-Life Building just beyond the slippery sidewalk.

Camilla clasped her computer bag, accepting the umbrella from the driver with a smile of thanks and, taking care not to slip on her four-inch heels, rushed after Talbot who was already in the grips of the revolving door. He was rustling around in his pockets a few feet from the lobby desk when she caught up to him.

"Forgot your ID?"

He nodded. "Left it at the office. This damn checking in."

"Let me try something. Can I have your phone?" She tapped out a quick text to Marcia, and a moment later had what she had asked for. She brought the phone to the front desk, slipping her own ID out from the wallet in her computer bag.

The guard, weary from a million self-important folks trying to bully him day in and day out, faced her stonily. "ID please."

She smiled and held out her own as well as the screen of Talbot's phone for the text with the shot, front and back, of his ID that Marcia had sent at her request. The guard took both. "Stand in front of the camera please."

He snapped her picture and handed both the phone and ID back along with one entrance badge. "You can go ahead, Miss Anderson, but the other guy, who may or may not be Mr. Talbot, better go on back home and get himself some ID. A picture of something 'aint that something."

Behind her, Mason observed, "That's a pretty arbitrary distinction that's eroding with the advance of technology. Consider Apple-Pay, for example, which is essentially a picture of cash, not the cash itself."

If looks could kill, it wouldn't matter that the guard

wasn't actually armed. Or she hoped he wasn't.

"This man is just doing his job," she said in a reproving tone.

The guard's nod in response to her sentiment was a step in the right direction. A line formed behind them.

"It's my first day," she confided as she returned her ID to her wallet, laughing in what she hoped would be construed as nerves, well, actually, really were nerves. "And this is my new boss." She leaned a little forward to the guard and added in a lower voice, "I'm sorry about this. We'll just have to go back to the office and get his ID. He probably thinks I should have reminded him about it. You know how that is. Anyway, it's just we have a flight after this and—"

She glanced back at the line and moved to the side, pulling Talbot with her, the solid muscle beneath the damp tweed slightly disconcerting. "But we're holding things up."

A man in a Burberry overcoat, five thousand dollar briefcase in hand, slapped his ID on the marble counter with an impatient huff. "I'm late for a meeting."

The guard eyed him before turning back to Camilla. "Let me see that phone again."

She complied and he took his time about it, staring at the screen, then at Talbot, the line getting longer and the raincoat guy's face getting redder.

"I guess this'll do."

One photo of the screen and one of Talbot and they had another entrance badge.

She grinned at the guard. "I appreciate it."

"This really your first day or you just say that to get me to help you?"

She laughed. "I would have if I had to. But no, it really

is my first day."

The guard smiled. "Good luck then."

When they boarded the crowded elevator, everyone shaking off like wet dogs, her unorthodox boss didn't push a button and Camilla asked, "What floor is the meeting on?"

"I have no idea."

The elevator ascended.

"You've never been to your outside counsel's?"

"I've been here a hundred times. I don't pay attention."

They stopped at sixteen to let a woman off. At seventeen somebody else.

"I'll call Marcia," he said.

Camilla shook her head, resolving to get a copy of the itinerary herself from now on. "I might have the firm name in my case." She started to fumble with the latch as the elevator moved up.

"Starts with a *B*," he offered. "Bingham. Bangum. Something like that."

A guy whose elbow was unintentionally crowding her asked, "Bannum Strauss?"

Her boss nodded. "That's it."

"You're in luck. You haven't missed it. Top floor."

The helpful guy pushed the button for them and got off to Camilla's thanks a few floors later. For the last leg of the ascent, even though the car stopped periodically at certain floors before getting to theirs for some reason, Camilla was alone with her boss.

"Speaking of social skills," she said, as gently as she could, "one of them is to say thanks."

"Thanks."

"Not to me. To the guard."

"Why? Wasn't that his job?"

"But he went out of his way to help us when you didn't have the right ID."

"Not until you smiled at him and acted all—" He stopped, as if he'd just made the connection.

"Nice? See, that's the point. That poor guy has people complaining all day about what he has to do, and 9/11 was *not* his fault."

"Someone said 9/11 was his fault?"

"No, I mean the security. Never mind. Just, you know what they say?"

"No idea."

"A little honey, right?"

He gave her a blank look, his gaze dipping to her neck. Was there something on her collar? She glanced down to discover fingers twirling her pearls. "Nervous habit," she said and dropped her hand to her side.

They both looked at the elevator door as they felt the car settling.

"And the good Samaritan who gave us the right floor. Wasn't he being nice? He deserved a thank-you, too, right?"

She felt ridiculous, like a kindergarten teacher.

"He was looking down your blouse."

"He was not!"

"Yes, he was. He was about my height. You were below us. I could tell."

So she guessed he noticed more things than he let on.

"Well, still."

The door opened to the floor they wanted, and he put his hand on her back to usher her out of the elevator, a politesse she wouldn't have expected along with a jolt at the physical contact, like when she put her hand on his arm before.

The elevator closed behind them to the massive glass doors of Bannum Strauss.

When they entered the spacious two-story lobby of the law firm, a sleek brunette behind the reception desk spread her raspberry red lips in a welcoming smile. "So nice to see you again, Mr. Talbot. I'll let Greg know you're here."

While she was dialing, Talbot wandered off to the floor-to-ceiling windows, hands behind his back. She didn't follow.

"Psst."

The receptionist crooked a finger at her, and Camilla went closer.

"You work for him?" she asked.

"As of today I do."

The brunette gave a furtive look his way. "I think he is *so* hot."

Camilla laughed. "Uh, okay."

"Come on, you have to admit it."

"I just work for him."

"Lucky you. One glance from those deep blue eyes and I was, like, *whoa*. The way he sort of looks right through you. I pray for Greg to schedule a meeting. Does he have a girlfriend?"

"Sorry. No idea. I just met him for the first time today. But, hey, give it a shot."

"As if. I've flirted as outrageously as I can, but he ignores me."

"Yeah, it seems like he's got a lot on his mind."

"I could really help him with his wardrobe sense."

"Who couldn't?" Camilla said, and they laughed, both looking over to where Talbot was shaking hands with a plump balding man who had descended on the circular central stairway in the lobby.

The two men met her at the desk, and Greg Porter introduced himself to Camilla, then led them to a conference room, saying he would let everyone else know Mr. Talbot was there.

Camilla looked around and took a seat at a walnut table that would not look out of place in the UN headquarters where they actually might need fifty places at a table.

Talbot paced around the room, ending up in front of the picture window, gazing down at the tiny building blocks of Manhattan through sheets of water and tapping his fingers against the glass in rhythm to the rain. He tackled the coffee on the sidebar next, pouring a cup with such a rattle he finally set it down, leaving it there, and resumed his stance at the window. She glanced at the half-filled cup, more liquid on the saucer than inside the rim. Had his hands been shaking? He had them in his pockets now, so she couldn't tell.

She hadn't noticed any of this restless energy in the limo, where he'd been all still and Spock-like. He almost looked nervous, though that would be ridiculous. As a CEO, he must be the veteran of dozens of these kinds of meetings.

"I wonder why we're in such a huge room," she mused. "I doubt there'll be more than ten people here."

"Not if I'm supposed to be here. It'll be a huge crew."

Jesus, he hated these dog and pony shows, as Marcia called them in the early days. He wished he could just send an email to the deal team, saying what he would pay and when he wanted to close and that would be the end of it from his perspective. But he'd been told time and time again that wasn't how it was done. Instead, he had to sit in on the first meeting, feeling as claustrophobic as ever by all the glad-handing, and let his lawyers posture for him and his bankers pretend they were giving him the deal of the century on the financing. There was a march to it all, and he felt distinctly out of step.

Had, ever since the very first meeting, years ago, when the company was no more than an idea on paper and a line of credit he had a slim chance of paying off without addition-al backers. Then, he and Marcia had cobbled together some half-ass presentations, no graphics even, and showed up in a room about as big as this, with an audience who had only given him an hour because his old professor from Caltech consulted on Wall Street and had rounded them up as a fa-vor. In exchange he promised the prof a quarter of one per-cent of the company, which had eventually enabled the guy to buy a sprawling ranch in Northern California, though he hadn't known it would at the time. Nobody believed in the idea except him and maybe Marcia.

Now he had a virtual army devoted to the cause, all of them wanting a piece of it. Mason glanced at his new law-yer, Camilla. Marcia was always trying to give him tricks to remember people's names, and for the most part he ignored them. The name came to him if it was important enough, and if it wasn't, well, enough said. But he suspected he wasn't for-getting this young woman's name. For one thing, she seemed very capable. Getting him through security without an ID, for example. If he'd been with Shreeman, he would have been yelling at Shreeman, who in turn would have been yelling at the guard and, in sum, they'd be a half hour late to the meeting because they had to go back to the office for some ID.

Which reminded him, he should have Marcia send a messenger with his driver's license out to the plane.

About to instruct Camilla, the thought went right out of his head as she smiled at him. She had been so, er, *nice* to the guard. Marcia was right. He probably could learn from her. She smiled an awful lot. It seemed to be her de facto facial expression. And when the odd fellow in the elevator had looked down her blouse, he was disturbed to find himself in sync with it. The swell of her breasts were just visible over the cream silk. And then the fucking pearls.

He could think of someplace else to put those. Draped over her bare breasts. Between her thighs.

He snapped his attention back to the window, trying to keep his mind off that kind of thing and on the deal at hand. Unfortunately, it didn't make him any more comfortable. It was silly really. There was no good reason to feel so ill at ease, so jittery that he couldn't pour a cup of coffee. He just needed to get through one more meeting.

But all it took was the memory of his first presentation, with one very memorable participant, to make his palms sweat at the prospect of sitting at a conference table. *She who shall not be named.* As one of his initial investors, she'd insisted on attending, poring over a pad of paper she had brought along, scribbling notes as if to correct him later on. He was probably the only wanna-be entrepreneur on Wall Street who was forced to bring his mother to his financing pitch.

When the presentation was over and the group still streaming out, she approached the podium and said as loudly as she could, "Well, that was a fiasco. Back to the drawing board I guess."

He had never enjoyed anything so much as writing her a check the next week out of the proceeds from the 100 percent investor participation after the meeting. Nothing had tasted as sweet as buying that woman the hell out of his company.

Even now, about to sit down to a meeting, he always had in the back of his mind the fear that his disapproving mother was going to show up.

The conference room door opened, and enough people to fill the UN-sized table flooded in. A crew, just as her boss had said. And every one of them, mostly middle-aged white men in suits, crowded in on Talbot in front of the window to introduce themselves. He was lost in a sea of handshakes and a flurry of business cards.

Camilla watched the fawning for a minute, but then on impulse rose from her seat and threaded her way through the gray suits. Half a dozen men leaned into her boss, all of them talking over each other with an intensity she heard before she got there. It almost looked like a football huddle, except wasn't the quarterback supposed to be giving the orders? Talbot stood stock-still, gaze fixed on a point just over the heads of the other men, alternated with looking at his feet.

"Mr. Talbot." Her voice was loud enough to cut through the chatter. She didn't know about social skills, but being in a large family had certainly taught her to project, as she'd proved in the limousine.

He raised his gaze, and though his eyes were hooded, she read relief in them. She gestured back to the table. "We're pressed for time. We should get started."

After holding one arm out, she shepherded her boss to his seat, putting herself between him and Porter, who talked in low tones to the man at his right.

Once everyone sat down, Porter assumed control of the meeting. "For the benefit of most of you here, and so you'll know who you're talking to on the next all-hands conference call, let's go around and introduce ourselves. I'm Greg Porter, Senior Partner at Bannum Strauss in Mergers and Acquisitions, and I'm the primary outside counsel for Talbot, Inc."

He went on to list the last five deals he'd done with Talbot, Inc. in some detail. When the lawyer finally finished and signaled they would go along the table counter-clockwise, she said, "I'm Camilla Anderson, inside counsel for Talbot, Inc."

She hoped with the one sentence to set the tone for brevity.

Everyone turned to Talbot, who was reading a few of the business cards he had been handed. There was an awkward silence. "Mr. Talbot," she said quietly. She could feel fifty pairs of eyes focusing on him.

One of the younger men in an expensive suit on the opposite side of the table broke into a tight, closed lip smile and whispered something into the ear of the clone next to him, who suppressed a chuckle.

"Oh, sorry." He scrunched his eyes, consulted the ceiling, fluorescent lights far above them, as if trying to remember.

"Mason Talbot," he said, and then he was back to the business cards, stacking them in tidy piles.

The man to the left of him did not carry on. In fact, everybody still zeroed in on the CEO, fascinated by the oddity of one of the rare species not taking the floor in a burst of exuberant confidence, all of them waiting to see what he would do next.

Remembering the spilled coffee on the saucer, Camilla jumped into the void. "You know," she joked, "the guy who'll be paying most of your bills?"

Polite laughter as she caught the eye of the man to the left of Talbot and prompted, "And you are?"

She didn't notice the rest of the names and bios so much as Talbot next to her reading those cards and scribbling on the back of each one, doodles when she looked closer, constantly adjusting and readjusting his position in his chair, jiggling his foot. Occasionally, he consulted the ceiling again.

A half hour later, as they were discussing the timetable, Talbot offered his first comment, to no one in particular, his eyes still on the cards. "This is wrong. I said I want to be done in a month. Not three."

Rustling of papers along the table and she took a quick look at the schedule for the deal on the handout they'd all been given. The timing did appear to be about a month too fat, if not more. "What is this long span in the middle for?" she asked the other participants. "It just says diligence. Why would it take four weeks to go through a data room?"

Porter responded to her in low tones. "We need to inspect the factories overseas. Standard procedure. What firm did you say you trained at?"

"Where are the factories? The moon?" she whispered

back.

Turning the pages of the handout, she said, louder, "No really. All kidding aside, where are the operations? It doesn't say."

Another gray suit down the table answered. "Eastern Europe mostly. But we're also hitting some investor meetings while we're over there. Western Europe primarily for those. Paris, Rome, London. Maybe Prague."

In other words, a boondoggle on Talbot's dime while he waited for his deal to close.

There was some uncomfortable shifting along the table as she left a long pause that indicated she knew it.

"I think we can whittle those four weeks down to one," she said with a smile. "Don't you?"

Talbot's phone rang, and after listening for a minute, he leaned over to whisper to her, his breath tickling her ear as she fought down the slight twinge of pleasure from the simple gesture. "We have to get out of here. Weather. Can you make the excuses?"

She nodded and he was out the door.

It took her another five minutes to make her exit, but when she got back to the limousine and climbed in, Talbot wasn't there. "Oh? Where is he?" she asked the driver.

"Didn't he leave with you?"

"Before me."

"No problem, miss. He must have turned the wrong way when he exited the building. He does that a lot. I'll look for him."

It was pouring outside, and Talbot didn't have an umbrella. About to hand the driver the one he'd given her, she said instead, "No, I'll go. I'm already damp. You stay here."

Umbrella hoisted to cover as much of her first-day best suit as possible, she walked back to the entrance and then rounded a corner of the building, catching sight of him half a block away, crouched down, his back to her. Hurrying along, wondering if he dropped something, she realized he was having a conversation—completely oblivious to the rain, forearms perched on his knees—with a homeless man sitting under a cardboard construction. Her billionaire boss who couldn't be bothered with an umbrella was drenched, and the man in the weathered army green jacket and scraggly beard was completely dry in his makeshift shelter. It must be cold for the poor man sitting on the wet ground, though. She wanted to give a donation, but then remembered she'd left her wallet in the car. Was that what Talbot was doing? She didn't see a container for money. Not even the usual sign. *Army Vet* or *Will work for food.*

The homeless situation in New York was so sad. She knew there were problems all over the nation, she and her sisters had always volunteered in soup kitchens in Detroit, but nowhere was the issue more visible than in the Big Apple, where people with more money than they knew what to do with stepped over others who didn't have any. Case in point with her new boss. Only he wasn't stepping over this man. He was talking to him.

"Mr. Talbot," she said when she reached him, trying to hold the umbrella over them both as he felt around inside his jacket, then in his outside pocket for something.

"Oh, here you go. Wait." He pulled back the business card he had just extracted to read it and then handed it to the guy. "No, it's mine. I have so many cards in there I wanted to make sure I wasn't giving you the number of a banker."

"That wouldn't do me no good," the man joked.

"They don't do anybody any good, Frank. No, that's my assistant's number, just call her and she'll set it up." He patted the top of the shelter, and thankfully it didn't come down on the man's head.

"Ingenious." Talbot stood, losing the protection of the umbrella, and turned to her. "Oh, there you are. I couldn't find the limousine."

"It's this way." She tried to keep on umbrella duty, holding it high enough for both of them, but he walked ahead, his long gait too fast for her.

He didn't say a word after they climbed into the limousine, the view out his window once again apparently impossible to miss.

As the limo pulled out into traffic with a jerk, she laid off the small talk. They could download about the meeting another time. Midtown traffic hadn't geared up to its climactic gargantuan fuck-up as yet, and the limousine had to run up on the curb of the expressway only once or twice to jump a slower vehicle. A smooth ride comparatively speaking. It was only twelve miles to Teterboro, the private airport where a corporate jet awaited.

In the muted light of the drizzle all around them, Talbot's face appeared paler than it had in the fluorescents, making his hair seem even darker, like a gypsy's with all its wild curls. If he looked at her, she felt sure his eyes would be an even deeper blue, contrasts all around. Like him to begin with.

"What were you doing with the homeless man?"

"Just admiring the construction of his shelter. It was three-plied. Very sturdy."

"He didn't pick a very good place to squat, though. Outside the Time-Life Building. The police will probably move him along. Can't have the tourists tripping over homeless folks. It's so sad."

He said nothing.

"Why did you give him your card?"

"I want him to work for me."

"Uh…really? Doing what?"

"Not sure yet. But building something like that, in the rain, no resources." He shrugged. "There are all different kinds of intelligences."

It was a sentiment everybody in her family had expressed, many times, and firmly believed. Not something she heard elsewhere, though, especially in this city where they worshiped at alters of elite degrees and bursting bank balances.

Talbot took out his phone and tapped on it, undoubtedly a text to Marcia about the man who would be calling her.

"His name was Frank," she offered, and he glanced up, smiling.

"I remember."

A warm sensation formed in the pit of her stomach.

When he put his phone away, he said, "I hate those big meetings, by the way. But they tell me my attendance is mandatory."

"It's a lot of posturing," she agreed. "They talk to hear themselves, while everybody's meter was running."

"So, Marcia says you're going to teach me some manners," he reminded her. "Actually, she sold it to me more like coping skills. In any case, you can start there because I feel as uncomfortable as hell in those types of situations, everybody trying to get at me. Makes me want to reach for the hand sanitizer."

She laughed.

"And I never have anything to say while they all look at me sort of accusingly for it. I don't give a shit, but…"

She wondered if that was true, her fingers automatically straying to her pearls. His eyes followed the motion. Maybe she'd sit on her hands.

"Well, we could try something, if you want. It worked in all my PR classes." And in her psychology class with certain phobias, though she declined to mention it. "You pretend I'm a stranger at a meeting, just like in there."

"You are a stranger. Pretty much."

"Right. But let's say I know you, by reputation of course."

"Don't you?"

She rolled her eyes, but one corner of his mouth came up, the dimple she'd noticed before making even the hint of his smile very attractive.

"Didn't you ever act out plays or anything when you were a kid with your siblings?"

"I don't have any siblings. That I know of."

"Oh." She'd walked right into that one. "Well, with friends then? Even if it wasn't actually a play, but more like cops and robbers or army sergeant and cadets?"

She and her sisters had played the military one. As the game was age-correlated, however, she was always relegated to cadet, being at the bottom of the brood. Such was life.

The dimple disappeared. "I didn't have many friends."

She coughed. "Well, that's a difficult time. Childhood, I mean. Or it can be."

She thought of the graceful old Tudor, three stories in all, where she had been raised, with faded hardwood floors and carpets beaten down under generations of little feet. Dogs that got bigger and more numerous each year, and cats that had litters before anybody even knew they hadn't been spayed, the kittens as tiny as mice when you perched them on your palm. Pure chaos. And tremendous fun.

She had loved her childhood, but not everybody was lucky enough to have warm enveloping protection all mixed in with rowdy camaraderie, and of course love.

"The important thing, Mr. Talbot, is you've made a success of yourself and of course you have friends now."

He opened his mouth and she forged on, determined he not correct her. "So let's role-play. I'll be that person trying to shake your hand and talk to you, and you think of something you want to say. No rush. No pressure. And next time you're in that situation, you won't feel at a loss. Let's try it."

She extended her hand, and though he looked doubtful, he took it, the blue eyes concentrating on her face, first only her eyes, but then he seemed to take a trip along the whole expanse, the cheeks, the hair, the chin. She suddenly wished she had worn more makeup, not the quick swipe of mascara and blush and the dab of glossy lipstick probably gone by now.

Unlike the brief handshake they had shared at his office, the prolonged clasp of his large, long-fingered hand over hers felt intimate. His breath seemed to come a little quicker. She knew hers did.

Seated opposite each other in the limo, they both leaned forward until they were only inches apart. She swallowed, remembering what it was she was supposed to be doing. "Ah, okay." She pasted a brighter smile on her glossless lips. "So, Mr. Talbot, I'm so honored to meet you. I've read all about your company and I think—um, let's make her—"

"Who?"

"The person I'm pretending to be. Let's make her an investment banker because they are the absolute, bar none, pushiest. So I've read about your company, and I think you're doing a fantastic job, but I know my firm could add fifty-whatever basis points to your stock and lower your debt cost a hundred-million basis points."

She pursed her lips at the exaggeration.

"Now, take your time, just think about it. I'm shaking your hand, pressing you for future business, whatever, and you say…"

She waited, and with the hand that wasn't shaking hers, he touched her strand of pearls, just one finger. So gently she almost thought she imagined it.

Then he said, "You have beautiful blue eyes."

Damned if that wasn't just what she was thinking!

# Chapter Two

She coughed. "Uh, well, uh…"

"Sorry." His voice was low. "It was what came to mind. Very light. Your eyes, I mean. But I guess that's not what I should say when I'm shaking hands with an investment banker, right?"

"No, that's okay. Everybody in my family has blue eyes. If one of us had brown," she babbled on, "that'd be a big deal."

He pulled his hand away and sat back, folding his legs, eyes on the window again. "It was just an observation."

"No, really, that's fine, Mr. Talbot. That's part of the role-playing. So we don't say the first thing that comes to our mind. You know, we practice."

"And I should have said what?"

"Well, something more generic like, 'I'm always open to new ideas. Feel free to give my secretary a call.' Then you could screen them and only talk to the ones you want."

"Very helpful. Thank you." But he was still looking out the window as the exit sign for the airport came up.

When they got to the airport and the car pulled up to the sleek private jet on the runway, two co-pilots hustled out to meet them holding umbrellas aloft to shield them from the driving rain. They grabbed Talbot's briefcase and her own roller suitcase, though she kept her computer bag.

"The weather's pretty bad, Mr. Talbot," one of them said as they climbed the steps to the plane. "But if you want to get to the UK today, we better go now."

"Fine," Talbot said shortly, taking one of the lush leather seats next to a window while she took another on the opposite side of the aisle after storing her bag in an upper bin.

"Miss White sent your wallet over as well." The pilot handed it to him.

"Thanks. I forgot to tell her to."

"I did," Camilla said. "When I asked for the picture of your ID."

He smiled at her slightly and slid the wallet into his back pocket.

After instructing them to buckle up for takeoff and warning they only had five more minutes for cell phones, the pilots disappeared behind the cockpit door.

Her cell rang and she saw her sister Carly's Westchester number.

"Go ahead, take it." He got out of his seat. "I want to run something by the pilots."

"Hi," she answered when he was gone.

"It's just your older sister bothering you on your first day."

"Which one?"

Carly pretended to be insulted. "The only one who was organized enough to have flowers delivered to your new office to celebrate your freedom from that horrible law firm!"

"Carly, you are so sweet."

"Did you get them before you left? I knew you'd only have them for a little while, since you're traveling, but I think it's important to have a special treat on your first day."

"Absolutely. They were gorgeous." She'd missed them at the office, but no need to spoil the thoughtful gesture.

"So, how is it?"

All in all, Camilla was feeling pretty good about the whole first day thing. Meeting? Check. Bonding with the boss? Getting there. Jetting off in a private plane? Double check. Who wouldn't rather take a trip to Europe with the boss instead of the usual first day tedium of learning where the office supplies were and waiting for IT to hook up your computer?

"Great," she summarized since she had at most five minutes. "But we're about to take off."

"Oh, you lucky girl. I was in London around ten years ago, and there was this sheik who was so attentive that—"

"Carly, I have to go, really. You are such a good sister to send me first-day flowers and call me."

"I know. I am. Be sure to tell Mom that when you talk to her. Tell her your big sis is looking out for you in the devil city until you can make your way home to your solid Midwestern roots. Never mind. I'll tell her myself."

She laughed. "I will, too. Now, I love you. Bye."

"Wait! No hustling me off the phone until you spill how the big boss is. He looked really cute in the profile I saw of him."

Despite that her boss clearly had a few quirks she could help him with, things were going to be okay between them. She could feel it. Stepping in for him at the meeting when he had shut down had felt natural, good. "I like him," she decided on.

"Well, I'm glad. But don't like him too much. He'll be sitting across from you in his fabulous plane in some perfectly tailored suit and giving you the eye."

Talbot came back down the aisle and resumed his seat, then kicked his gym shoes off.

"Not exactly. But I have to go. We're about to take off."

"Be good. And remember no imbibing to excess. You know that always makes you too flirty, and that is not the first impression you want to be giving."

"Of course. Don't be silly."

"Hey, I remember Reno."

That was the thing with sisters. They remembered everything, in this instance one wild night when she found out she passed the bar and she and three of her sisters, Brandy, Dee Dee, and Carly, flew to Reno on the spur of the moment. Not a good idea in retrospect. The headache pounding at her temples the next day from the tequila shots could have shaken the scenic mountains outside the window of their hotel. And some guy named Franz who she absolutely didn't remember kept sending her completely inappropriate emails for weeks thereafter, though thank God her sisters assured her she'd never been alone with him.

Carly added, "Although it's good to let go sometimes. So don't be too hard on yourself if you do."

"There's a mixed message if I've ever heard one."

"Nuanced, not mixed."

She smiled. "Okay, I will. I mean I won't. I promise. Got to go."

She hung up and glanced at Talbot to see if he had been listening to that last part, but he gave no indication, and in minutes the plane was headed into the clouds, the altitude allowing them to escape the storm. Early afternoon sunlight filtered through the tufts of white dotted here and there outside the window.

Talbot extracted a magazine from his briefcase and began to read it. Apparently, he'd had enough small talk. She couldn't blame him. That was probably more than he'd had in the last year. She stood up to get her iPad from the overhead where she had stashed her computer bag, and the plane lurched unexpectedly, forcing her to grab on to his seat back to steady herself. Her fingers brushed his hair, and he looked up at her. She'd been to St. Martin once, and that was what his eyes reminded her of. The cobalt Caribbean sea washing over her. His hair was silky, and she wondered how it would feel to run her hands through it, to feel it against her cheek. She let go of his seat. "Sorry about that."

After locating the iPad as fast as possible, she sat back down.

For the first time since she'd been introduced to him, his intense stare made her feel self-conscious. Maybe it was the nice eyes comment or that almost-there touch to her pearls in the limo that she was thinking she must have imagined. He watched her steadily. Since they were the only passengers on the six-hour flight, and he was proving to be staring-prone, she supposed she was in for a lot of that.

Camilla tried not to take it personally as her new boss

cocked his head and studied her like she was one of the chips in the thing-a-ma-jiggy he'd invented and built his fortune selling. *Thing-a-ma-jiggy.* With that kind of know-how, little wonder she'd gone to law school. But you didn't need to know a product to do M&A.

"I might not have said this before, but I'm really excited to be joining your company and to have this opportunity to work for you."

Now that it was just the two of them, he really should be asking her to call him by his first name. She was about to suggest it, more of that etiquette training, when he said, "Listen, do you think we could, you know, have sex? I could pay you extra of course. I know it's not part of your job, but I'd love to strip you bare to just those pearls and bury myself in your—"

"What?" Only it came out more like a squeak. Enough to stop him in his tracks, though.

*Of all the...!* Fury pounded through her veins, shock and embarrassment and white-hot anger coursing through her, all at the same time. As soon as she got over the stun-gun effect of it, she was going to tell him what to do with that question, etiquette be damned.


The little lawyer's mouth dropped open. That was Mason's first clue. Her creamy complexion turned bright red. Okay, that was his second. She wasn't even playing with her pearls anymore, for which he was grateful, since she'd been turning him on with the casual gesture all afternoon. But that shriek. He might have made a mistake.

"I don't mean anything by that. If you don't want to, don't worry about it. It's not a big deal."

For a minute, she appeared speechless. Then she said, "You don't need a corporate lawyer, you need an employment lawyer."

"Why? I'm employed."

"You just propositioned me."

"Is that illegal or something?"

"Yes. It is."

"Oh, well, that's why they invented lawyers, I guess. So you could point that kind of thing out."

She stood up, looking around as if she needed to find the exit. Good luck with that. They were a mile high. He glanced back down to the trade magazine he had brought along to read, more disappointed than he cared to admit. The suggestion may have been spur of the moment, but he had fiercely wanted her to say yes, a little dazzled by her warmth, drawn to her and hoping she had been attracted to him. "No, really." Her voice climbed a decibel. "You can't say that kind of thing."

He nodded absently, looking up in surprise when she snatched his reading material away and his hands clasped on empty air.

She glared down at him. "Is this what Marcia meant by teaching you social skills?"

"I don't think so."

"The Spock thing isn't cutting it anymore. To think I had just been feeling so warm and fuzzy about my first day."

"Warm and fuzzy? I'm not sure I—"

She shook a finger at him. "I need this job. So I'm going to ignore what you said, personally speaking, and not slap your face so hard it'll make your head spin worse than *The Exorcist*."

Although he rarely understood pop cultural references, he got that one. But she meant the girl possessed by the devil in the movie, not the exorcist himself. It was the *girl* who was writhing around, her head spinning and so on. He knew a thing or two about that at this very second.

"Calm down."

"Don't you tell me to calm down!" But she took a deep breath and said in a more modulated voice, "I'm advising you, *as* your lawyer, that you can't proposition employees."

He looked at her, tilting his head, wrinkling his brow. "Even for money?"

"Especially for money!"

He shrugged. "Well, I don't see why not. I'm paying you to be here anyway, aren't I?"

"Look, I don't know if you're teasing me—" She scrutinized him for a second then added, "And I sense you're not. But just don't blurt out things like that. You're the CEO of a public company."

"If you won't have sex with me, can I have my magazine back?"

She flung it behind her with vigor worthy of the first pitch in the one or two ballgames he had actually watched. *Guess not.* Maybe he should get the Annual Report out of his briefcase and turn back to that.

"Talking like that is *completely* inappropriate. Why would you even think you could say something like that?"

He tried to remember why he had said it. It was the pearls maybe. "You don't look like one of my normal employees. Except for the suit and everything. You look like a woman

I'd want to have sex with."

"You jerk!"

"How am I being a jerk by wanting to have sex with you?"

"You're being a jerk by saying so."

"Even if it's true?"

"Yes!" She paced up and down the narrow aisle of the jet, hugging her arms to her slender frame.

"Even if I'm thinking it?" he persisted.

"Yes. For instance, I'm not saying right now that I think you're the biggest asshole boss I've ever come across in a long, long line of asshole bosses."

"I think you *did* just say it."

She paused to confront him. "Is there something wrong with you?"

He settled back in his seat. "Like what? I'm horny right now, but otherwise I'm okay."

"First I'm supposed to teach you social skills or good manners or some shit and now this? I'm a lawyer. Not some Martha Stewart sex-for-hire, I don't know what."

"That's a horrible image. I actually had a meeting with her once so I know what she looks like."

She went back to pacing and tossed over her shoulder, "Everybody knows what she looks like."

"Really? Well, she looks nothing like you."

"I'm here to give you legal advice. I thought we were getting somewhere."

"It doesn't look like it," he said under his breath.

"Just because I'm a woman," she muttered, "you think you can talk to me like this?"

"Well, I wouldn't want to have sex with a man. I'm not wired that way. Especially not that Shreeman punk." He adjusted his chair to semi-reclining. "What a whiner."

"Incredible."

"*You're* kind of whining now, though. But the thing is you've got an awesome chest—"

"Enough!" The carpet was taking a beating from her pointy shoes, but she took deep breaths, seeming to reach for some kind of higher power calm as she walked back and forth. Which was fine with him. He didn't appreciate lawyers, or anybody really, freaking out on him. And he didn't feel like yelling at her, as just the very sight of Shreeman for some reason had made him want to do. So far, she had been kind of sweet, in the limo with her role-playing and watching out for him at the meeting. She was easy to talk to, even for him.

It was...*nice.* He...*liked her.* He turned the unusual phrases over in his mind.

Coaching him through small talk seemed brave of her as well, even if Marcia had instructed her to do it. She struck him as a person who was very level-headed, sensible. Well, not at this particular minute. He was getting dizzy following her with his eyes. He watched her make short work of the length of the plane, again and again, up and then down in no time, arms crossed as if she was freezing.

And of course she was sexy as hell. Her ass, which he hadn't had an opportunity to observe as she had, for the most part, been walking beside him or behind him or sitting across from him, was, he saw as she paced, high and rounded in her straight skirt. It looked as plush as her breasts.

He still felt like having sex with her, as a matter of fact, despite this odd conversation. But he supposed that was totally off the table.

"Are you trying to offend me?" she asked quietly.

"No."

She stopped her incessant pacing, putting the brakes on at his seat. "Upset me?"

"No."

She braced her arms on the overhead above him. "Push me around somehow?"

"No."

"In some sicko-power trip kind of way or anything?"

Even with the elaboration, it was a no. He shook his head.

She backed off. "So there *is* something wrong with you?"

"I guess. Can I have my magazine back now?"

Mason Talbot was supposed to possess some kind of astronomical IQ. That must be what the problem was.

Camilla had never dated a genius. But even the densest guy knew he needed a filter. That he couldn't let whatever sexist, horn-dog thoughts he was having make it directly up to his mouth. Even the dumbest guy knew that!

Not the smartest guy, though, apparently.

It was one thing for her to think her boss was cute and chat with the receptionist about flirting with him. That was just her being a girl for God's sake. No harm done. Even for him to tell her she had nice eyes wasn't a big deal.

But *quid pro quo*, straight out like that? To go to the nuclear option, boss-wise, right to her face! Not locker room talk behind her back, which she knew went on and didn't offend her any more than she suspected her girlish gab would offend him.

But to just ask her like that, straight-faced, as if it was okay to put her in that position?

*On her first fucking day!*

She didn't know in which capacity she was more horrified, as a twenty-first century product of decades of feminism and member of an extremely girl-powered family…or as his lawyer.

"I'm surprised you don't have a string of sexual harassment suits against you a mile long," she muttered, retrieving his magazine and flinging it back at him. He took it with a disinterested glance her way and set back to reading as she resumed her seat.

"And you can't fire me as a result of this," she added fast. "You know at least that much, don't you?"

"I never fire anyone," he said without looking up. "Sometimes I tell Marcia to make sure I don't see somebody again, but I think she just transfers them. Or doesn't. I haven't wanted to see Shreeman for quite some time, but he kept showing up."

"Well, let me be clear, Mr. Talbot, that you can't fire a woman for turning down sex with you."

"Why would I?"

He was still not looking up, talking in that same disinterested tone.

She scoffed. "Because your ego's bruised, that's why."

He raised his head finally and gave her a bewildered look. "What does my ego have to do with it?" Then he continued reading.

"*Do* you have a string of sexual harassment suits against you?" She didn't see anything mentioned when she did the

Google search on him, but she supposed with his money he could hush it up. Hard to believe Shreeman would've passed up the opportunity to throw that into his diatribe, but maybe he took his non-disparagement agreement more seriously than she thought. "I need to be prepared from a litigation perspective at the very least. Is this *quid pro quo* part of your regular working atmosphere? Because if so, it's going to stop right now and we're going to settle—generously, I might add—with any woman who has a claim against you."

"Mr. Talbot," she prompted when he didn't respond.

"Hmmm? Oh, a claim for what?"

"Sexual harassment," she said as calmly as she could. She felt as if she had wandered into a John Grisham novel and the reputable place she'd come to practice law was suddenly revealed to be a den of iniquity.

He put down his magazine finally. "Are we still talking about this?"

"We are."

"So tell me again. What is it? It's sexual harassment to ask a woman to have sex with you? Because I think I have done that before. Usually at some excruciatingly boring function I have to go to. Although what if it's them asking?"

It was hard to tell if he was being purposefully obtuse. She had known smart people who couldn't change a light bulb. Maybe he was challenged like that.

"No," she explained patiently. "It's sexual harassment to ask an *employee* to have sex with you."

"For money, right?"

"No. At all."

"Where does the money figure in?"

"Forget about the money. How many times have you

asked an employee to have sex with you? How many potential claimants are we talking about?"

"Once. One."

"What?"

"You. Right now. Remember when I—"

"I remember!" she said. "But are you trying to tell me I'm the first employee you ever asked to have sex with you?"

"I'm not trying to tell you that. I am telling you that because you asked me."

Well, that was good. From a litigation perspective. If he was telling the truth. But bad, too.

Like she needed this. She had student loans to pay off. "If you don't mind me probing a little further here, why did you suddenly ask me?"

"Didn't we go through this before? I find you attractive. Whatever. It was only a thought."

"Well, you've made it very awkward for me."

"Why?" he said in an exasperated tone and dropped the magazine on his lap.

"Because now I know you're thinking about having sex with me."

"Not anymore."

"This *is* some kind of weird mind-game shit, isn't it?"

"No, but you're acting very oddly."

"*I'm* acting oddly?"

"Didn't I just say that?"

She did a quick mental inventory of her outstanding loans, the sheer size of the remaining principal helping her regain her equilibrium.

She could put up with a lot. And he wasn't attacking her or anything. In fact, he seemed to have lost interest in the whole subject. Maybe this was just the female equivalent of screaming at Shreeman, which wasn't fair, but hey, that was life. Kind of like having an idiot savant for a boss.

He watched her, as if waiting for her to continue the discussion, or conclude it. Now might be the best time to set down some ground rules.

"Fine, Mr. Talbot, I'm willing to disregard your irregular, well actually *illegal*, suggestion."

"It's still hard for me to believe that's illegal," he pointed out.

"Well, it is."

He shrugged. "I guess you'd know."

"But it will continue to make things awkward for me if you refer to it again."

"You're the one who keeps talking about it."

"Because I want to make sure you understand," she snapped.

"Fine. I got it. Just so I know, though, if you weren't my employee, would you have sex with me?"

"No," she said automatically, not sure it was true, but really, really sure she shouldn't encourage that line of thought.

"Because you're not biologically attracted to me?"

If she didn't know better, she would swear there *wasn't* an ounce of ego, or rancor for that matter, in his question.

Who was this guy?

There hadn't been any personal details in the bios she'd read—other than the interesting fact that his father had been an anonymous sperm donor—but she was suddenly unbearably, and unwisely, curious.

He seemed remarkably clueless.

And, what with that Byronic thing going on, just a little

bit adorable as a result. Which was just so wrong.


In retrospect, Mason was sorry he'd brought the whole thing up. But he had, and Camilla seemed to be having quite an adverse reaction to the whole subject. And they had been getting along so nicely. He wished he'd thought to mention this possibility to Marcia. She would have warned him off the whole idea.

He hadn't realized how long it had been since he had sex until he finally looked at the *suit* or rather beyond the suit, as she insisted on making conversation and was so helpful at the meeting. And then those pearls. Something about the sheen against her pale skin made him want to shove himself inside her, deep, deep inside, and feel the silk of her thighs against his palms, bury his face in her neck, both of them shiny with sweat as they moved against each other.

His breath came faster.

Most people he saw through a sort of film, and he didn't care to peel it back. But from the beginning he *saw* Camilla. And then once on the plane and sitting across from her, completely alone except for the out of sight pilots, the thought just came to him. He could take her shiny blond hair down from the knot she had it in and run his fingers through the mass. He could —

He stopped. Apparently, he couldn't.

He had a great respect for biology, once it kicked in, and he knew what he was feeling was a powerful attraction. However, she didn't appear to be feeling the same. A damn shame. With her smiles and the easy flow of the conversation, he had thought she might. Just to be sure, though, he had asked her outright.

"You're asking if I'm attracted to you?" she responded.

"Yes." Since she had gone to Harvard, he wouldn't have thought she was slow, but she did seem to be repeating his questions back to him quite a bit.

"I don't want you to take this the wrong way, but this awkwardness in your social skills, does it extend to sexual matters?"

"Quite possibly. I don't consult Marcia on the specifics of that."

"Thank the Lord for small favors," she muttered. "Okay, then I'm going to give you the benefit of the doubt and assume that you're not continuing this conversation and asking me whether I'm attracted to you because you're getting some kind of perverted thrill out of keeping the sex talk going."

"I don't feel the slightest bit thrilled by the fact you won't have sex with me."

"*And* I'm going to take it at face value that you honestly don't know that asking me whether I'm attracted to you is inappropriate, like asking me to have sex was."

"Really?"

She nodded.

"But the blue eyes thing, in the limo, that was okay? You didn't freak out at that."

"Not okay exactly, but more like harmless."

There seemed to be an awful lot of rules around this whole thing. "I guess you really are going to have to teach me about small talk."

"Small talk, not sex talk. Dial 1-900-whatever for that."

No clue as to what she meant by the numerical reference, he said, "Well, is there anything I can ask you?"

"You can ask me about my credentials. Or about the job. And we can work on getting you to feel more relaxed in social settings and at big meetings."

"I meant about having sex together."

"No." She hesitated then said, "Does this approach usually work for you? Just putting it out there like that. *Got sex?* You know."

"Why do you get to ask that? Isn't that asking me about sex?"

"You're right. I shouldn't have."

"That's fine. I was simply pointing out the internal inconsistencies in your line of questioning. I don't mind answering you at all. The fact is I believe in being straightforward about most things. Which reminds me, I know you're a lawyer, like Shreeman was, but what do I need a lawyer on this trip for? Specifically, I mean. Not the social skills or whatever, although you have been very helpful on that score."

"You're negotiating a potential acquisition in London."

"I know. But that'll be just me and the other principal. Not a big side show like back in New York."

"I'm along to hear the discussion so I can begin to draft the contract if it gets to that stage." She added in an undertone, "I didn't know letting you spend six hours between my legs on the way over was part of the deal."

He arched an eyebrow.

"What, did I shock you?"

"You did if you thought I could last six hours."

She shook her head. "I guess you are straightforward."

Mason usually didn't like talking to women. Well, to anyone most of the time, really. But for some reason he didn't mind conversing with Camilla, in the limo, before the meeting, here in the plane. Maybe he thought it *would* end up with him getting between her legs. Or maybe he was just disappointed with the in-flight reading choices.

Or maybe… He, uh, he *liked* her.

The new boss didn't seem to have asked if she was attracted to him in a sleazy way, just because he wanted to know. Despite moving on, his question hung there between them, and she couldn't ignore it.

"As for your earlier question, biological attraction doesn't have anything to do with it, Mr. Talbot."

He did a double take. "That's not accurate. Biological attraction is the basis for sexual relations."

She went over to a metal cabinet near the cockpit door that had a bunch of drawers in it. After opening one, she saw packages of peanuts and chips and rows of candy bars. Passing on those, she tried another and found what she was looking for. A baby bottle of scotch was clearly called for. It wasn't five o'clock where they'd come from, but it was where they were going. The sun was coming in a little dimmer now, too.

And as to Carly's warnings? Her sister would certainly understand why Camilla was being driven to drink here. Anybody would. Carly was never going to believe this story. Actually, maybe she wouldn't tell any of her sisters. It depended on whether she decided to keep the job.

But, hell, she had to keep the job! At least until she

got another one. There was no grace period on her loans for bosses who were clueless about the basic fundamentals of the modern workplace. A compliment was awkward but fine. A raw invitation to fuck the big boss...for money...on her first day...was *so* not.

Even if she was a little tempted. Not the money part of course, but the —

*Hold on, girl!* She could almost hear Carly or any one of her other sisters, all of whom would be shocked down to their highlighted roots at the concept of sleeping with the boss. And don't even start on her mother.

This was not a fantasy. This was real. Her career was at stake. Maybe even modern feminism.

She twisted the cap off the miniature liquor bottle.

Although it was kind of unfair to put the whole burden of modern feminism on *her* shoulders.

She poured the scotch into a crystal cut glass and held another bottle out his way. "Want one?"

"No. Alcohol destroys brain cells."

"No problem there. I think you could use a few less." She dropped his mini-bottle back in the drawer, closed it, and took a healthy first sip of her scotch. Actually, kind of a gulp. "I have to be honest here. I know the rich are different and everything, and eccentric is one thing, I mean I was starting to like you — "

"You were?"

"But now that you've crossed the line, I'm not sure how this is going to work."

"What?"

"This. Us."

"I thought you said we couldn't have sex together."

"Working! Working together, I mean."

"Oh. Whatever."

His casual dismissal annoyed her. "And I kind of resent it. This is my first day. Don't they have HR training or something at this company?"

"Mmmm."

He was looking at her with those really cute blue eyes and, *goddamit*, this was all reminding her that she'd had quite a dry spell herself. The plane took a little jolt, turbulence or something again, and she grabbed for the side of one of the seats, her drink spilling onto the aisle. He popped up to steady her, surprisingly gallant. With his big hands resting on the slight swell of her hips, his breath warm at her temple, she felt a twinge in the pit of her stomach. More minor than a thrill. Far from being turned on. But still it was there.

She raised her gaze, and he dropped his hands to pick up the spilled drink and set it on the counter.

The plane steady again, she helped herself to a fresh bottle. After all, she'd barely started on the last. Since they were heading east, the light outside the window was growing fainter by the second. Or maybe the storm was catching up with them.

He sat back down and so did she across the aisle from him again. He picked up his magazine, and she tended to her scotch, relishing the smoky taste of a very good brand.

After a few minutes, she said, "I'm sorry but I still feel like I need to clear the air here. Are you always this blunt in coming on to women or is it just me again?"

He put down his magazine. "I heard you about no sex. I'm sorry I even mentioned it."

"Well, me, too."

"I just haven't had it in a while, and you reminded me of that. Okay? Simple enough. Just drop it."

She finished off the almost-second scotch, and the buzz it gave her made her less likely to try to treat this whole situation as just another bizarre thing bosses were apt to want you to do. Like working all night proofreading impossibly convoluted merger agreements for deals that probably weren't going to close the next day anyway. Or writing endless memos on legal strategies that anybody with a brain in their head could see were stupid from the get-go.

Like that.

"I see," she said. "So, since you're not getting any, or not much anyway, being with me made you think maybe you could fit some in during the flight, is that it?"

"Well, kind of. But that was probably a trick question, right?"

"See, you're not as clueless as you seem." She resisted the impulse to get up for another scotch and said sullenly, "Anyway, don't you have a girlfriend or something? God, you're rich enough."

"There's a necessary correlation?"

"Please! You might actually not know what sexual harassment is— And I'm still not sold on that."

He shrugged.

"But you can't possibly be naive enough not to know that rich guys can get whoever they want."

"I'm not naive. I just work a lot," he pointed out.

"To the exclusion of everything else probably."

"Most people don't," he hesitated, "*interest* me."

"Oh, I forgot. Because you're a genius, right?"

"I don't like labels."

"Look, I didn't get my Ph.D. at twenty-five and make a killing in an IPO or anything, but I'm not stupid here."

"Are you talking about the shirt? It was the only thing I could put on that was clean."

"What?"

"Never mind."

"So do you think it's easy to get into Harvard and graduate cum laude?"

"For some people, probably not."

She stopped short and lost the battle on the scotch front, getting up to get another one after all and pouring two of the mini-bottles into the glass for good measure and some ice. All right, three doses of the liquid courage.

"I must say, though, it would be impossible for me to go to law school. If I had to read legalese all day, I'd go nuts."

When she sat down, she muttered, "You're already there. And you *can* fire me for that, by the way."

"Why?"

"It's disrespect. Calling you nuts."

"I told you, they don't let me fire anyone. They don't let me give interviews, either."

"Now, that one makes sense."

He did that head cocking thing again. "Have you had sex before?"

"Me? Of course I have! What kind of a question is that?"

"You just seem extremely shocked by the suggestion we have it."

"It's the context."

"I see."

She shouldn't say it. She really shouldn't. She took another drink of the scotch, which got smoother with every swallow. But hell, he'd been blunt enough with her. Her turn.

"I do like your looks, though. I was thinking that just before you opened your mouth and blew everything all to hell by asking to fuck me."

"Yes, I see now that was a mistake."

"I'm glad I managed to get that through to you."

"You were very clear."

Camilla drank her liquor and looked at him, lovely still, but her pale blue eyes a little glassy. Her tidy bun was somehow messier now, too, and the blond wisps around her face made her look more attractive, not less. She started to play with the damn strand of pearls around her neck again. She was purposely trying to drive him crazy now. He was convinced.

"I could never sleep with my boss," she said in what must have been the twentieth variation on that same theme since he had brought the subject up. "It's so retro and really wrong. I mean, who does that?"

He didn't know what the retro referred to, but he supposed the whole practice hadn't been as frowned upon in the past as it apparently was now. Again, a pity. But as to the wrong, well, she had been abundantly clear on that score.

And he had stopped thinking about it. Absolutely. Almost.

"We're not in some episode of *Mad Men*, are we?" she demanded.

"I don't think so."

"Although I would sleep with that Don Draper, I don't care who he was. Any girl would. Don't let anybody tell you different."

He didn't know who Don Draper was, but he was jealous.

"And that's not a mixed message, by the way. It's *nuanced*."

The word came out slightly slurred, but in a cute way.

"I mean, we're allowed to fantasize, right?"

She took the words right out of his mouth, although he *had* caught on by now that he wasn't supposed to say them. He was fantasizing about her right at this very second. How the glossy pearls she was playing with would look against her bare cleavage with no blouse impeding the full effect.

When she took her suit jacket off suddenly and tossed it onto the seat next to her, he got an even better view of those breasts.

"Thirty-four *D*," she volunteered wryly at his undoubtedly focused stare. The piece of information went straight to his crotch.

He was pretty sure her disclosure of bra size was squarely in the list of things they weren't supposed to talk about — sexual body part measurements — but he certainly didn't mind the internal inconsistency in her line of thinking now. And no way was he going to point it out to her.

"If this was my fantasy," she said off-handedly, "do you know what I'd do?"

"No."

She set the empty glass on the seat next to her, nestling it in her suit jacket.

"I'd climb on your lap and kiss you."

# Chapter Three

He said nothing and she scoffed.

"And if you were a normal guy, you would've responded to me *saying* that by *you* saying 'go ahead.' Egging me on kind of. Get it?"

"No. But go ahead. I like this role-playing a lot more than the kind we were doing in the limo."

Her tight smile only opened up after a second or so, as if she was trying to stifle it and wasn't able to.

"You are pretty cute. But if this is some kind of lame move you use with women, I'm going to be really mad. Like Tony Curtis in *Some Like it Hot*, where he puts on that Cary Grant accent and pretends he can't get it up so Marilyn Monroe will fall all over him trying to 'cure' him."

"I never said I couldn't get it up."

She leaned over the aisle with a wicked smile and placed her hand on his knee, causing him to suck in his breath trying to hold off a groan. "I'd say you're proving that right now."

He glanced down to his trousers where his cock was standing to attention, following the conversation avidly. "Is it possible to get back to talking about you climbing onto my lap?"

"Possible. Not probable. I'd need a few more scotches for that."

He frowned.

"What?" she demanded, taking her hand off his knee. "Don't tell me you're going to quibble about that! Listen, your best bet is for me to get so plastered I don't even remember who you are. Then maybe you'll score."

That scenario didn't appeal to him.

"What is *that* look for? You're okay with pressuring an employee into sex, but not with getting her drunk to do it? How does that make sense?"

"I wasn't pressuring you. I only asked."

"Which since you're my boss constitutes undue pressure under the law."

"Well, I didn't know that. Now I do."

"But drunk girls give you pause. Why is that?"

"Alcohol not only kills brain cells, it can impair judgment."

"Why don't you look into heavy debt loads impairing judgment, too? That's why I'm still a lawyer."

"How long have you been a lawyer?"

"Five years. Which is four years and three hundred and sixty-four days too long."

"I see."

"I didn't mind being sworn into the bar and taken out to lunch on my first day of practicing, but it's all been downhill since then."

He laughed, which surprised him. He didn't do too much

of that usually, too intent on keeping his eye on his career, on building his company, and too little time for much else.

"And for the record," she added, "I haven't been laid in almost that whole time if you can believe it. Or at least the last two-thirds."

"Why not?"

"Too busy. Too tense. Too I don't know what. Did your mom really use a sperm bank to conceive you?"

Not sure he liked the abrupt change in subject—he'd rather try to steer her back to the subject of getting laid—he went along anyway. "Yes. She did."

He didn't know why everyone always seemed so interested in the sperm bank aspect of his parentage. He had said it during his first interview with the *New York Times* for some reason, he couldn't remember why, and the suit who was handling the reporter had scowled at him at the time and made annoying hand signals that involved fingers going in a horizontal line across his neck. It was very distracting. Of course that was before the PR department stopped allowing any interviews with him altogether, which was fine with him. But people still brought it up to him from time to time. "Apparently, my mother's criteria were very specific."

"Only genius sperm?"

"I don't think so. She wasn't very intellectual."

Her mouth dropped open. "I can't believe that. Who was your sperm donor then? Albert Einstein?"

He shrugged. "I have no idea."

"When was the last time *you* had sex?" she asked, which he definitely took as the conversation going back in the right direction.

"I couldn't pinpoint the time for certain, but more recent

than you I'm pretty sure."

"You're probably not very good in bed," she said, almost to herself, and then added, to him, "How could you be? Being how you are, I mean. Clueless. Probably slam-bam-thank you-ma'am. No offense."

"None taken."

Though he was kind of annoyed at how casually she was discussing this now. He could barely breathe with wanting her, and his cock was aching to show her *how he was in bed* while she was still fiddling with the fucking necklace.

"I tell you what," he said. "Let's role-play and you can see for yourself."


At first Mr. Genius-Inventor clearly did not have the slightest idea how to flirt. She kept giving him softballs, and instead of responding with "why don't you see" or "you be the judge," he kept answering her straight-faced.

But the role-playing line was pretty good. It shot a bolt of excitement through her right down to between her legs. The intensity of his glittering blue eyes didn't help, one curly black lock falling over his forehead. She wanted to either kiss his eyes closed or lose herself in them. Anything. If she just waited, she was going to die or explode. Or maybe even do something really, really stupid that she wouldn't be able to blame on the scotch later because she wasn't *that* drunk.

"Maybe we could start with one kiss," she barely breathed. "Do you like to kiss?"

"Yes," he said, his voice gravelly. "I've been thinking about kissing you all day as a matter of fact. Wondering what you'd taste like."

They leaned closer to each other over the aisle, and he linked his fingers in her string of pearls and tugged.

*God.*

His lips closed over hers slowly, carefully, his palm cupping her neck, the slight pressure just enough. One light kiss and then a second until she leaned farther in and opened her lips to him. He held her still for a long, thorough kiss, his lips firm against hers, his tongue delving in, tangling with her own in little thrusts she felt between her legs. He tasted minty and delicious.

She tried to steady herself, reaching out while they kissed, and landed a handful of his silky hair, grasping it, rocked by the sensations flooding through her. He shuddered and broke away with a groan, his blue eyes so dark they were almost black now, and her hands dropped to her lap, feeling suddenly empty.

"How was that?" he asked softly.

She cleared her throat. "Good. Pretty good. Nice actually."

"I can do better." He cupped her head again, sifting his fingers through her hair, loosening the bun even more, tingles shooting through her at the subtle massage. "Let's try again."

His mouth was rougher this time, and his five o'clock shadow lightly scraped her cheek. He kissed like he really had been thinking of it all day. Long greedy swipes of his tongue that made her hips arch in her seat even while she twisted to the side and strained to get closer, her own tongue exploring the warm wet depths of his mouth. When he pulled away a second time, her heart was beating fast against her chest, her breath uneven and her cheeks hot from more than just the razor burn. For a moment, she forgot who he was and who she was and wanted nothing so much as to climb right over the aisle and close the distance between their bodies.

He leaned back. "Better?"

She nodded, not trusting herself to speak.

"To really make any further progress, Camilla, you need to come over to this side of the plane."

She swallowed hard and started to get up, veering toward the liquid courage. "Let me get another scotch."

He grabbed her hand to stop her. Even that slight touch felt good. His thumb circled her palm in a mesmerizing motion as she stood in the aisle. "No more scotch if we're going to play this game."

She looked down at him. His jacket was still on, and needless to say, so were his pants, but a quick glance at his lap showed the heft of him straining toward her. His hair was mussed from her fingers, his breathing shallow and his dilated pupils partially shaded by those long black lashes. He was as excited as she was.

"I don't know," she said. "I'm not supposed to play this game with you."

"I got that. But sometimes you have to break the rules, don't you?"

His voice was even lower than it usually was, and she leaned down slightly to hear him over the noise of the plane. His mouth was only an inch or so from her breasts, the nipples erect, straining through the silk, and she willed him to press his lips against the thin material. Just the thought of it sent her pulses racing. Instead, he reached behind her and unclasped her pearls before taking them in one hand and running the beads along the length of her neck, a soft sensuous feeling.

She didn't break the rules. Not usually.

He brought her palm to his lips, pressed a light kiss on it, and dropped the pearls in her hand, then closed it with his own. "If we're going to stop, you'd do me an immense favor if you'd put these away."

She could stop. She could still stop.

She lowered her hand, astounded by her audacity, and lightly skimmed the pearls against his hard cock, feeling the heat right through his pants. He groaned and closed his eyes for a second, and she unconsciously arched her hips, imagining him inside her, deep and hard.

She turned her hand slowly, the pearls spilling out, and his cock jerked and seemed to swell even further, like a living thing begging to be freed. One side of his mouth came up, dimple in full evidence, and he clasped her wrist, holding it slightly away. "I'm dying here, Camilla."

A girl could break the rules once in a while, couldn't she?

"Show me," she whispered.

He tugged her toward him, the pearls tumbling to the carpet, until she was sideways in his lap, his desire for her solid beneath her bottom. Holding her in one arm, cradled, he kissed her hotly, and with the other hand he explored, a touch at her neck, then her collarbone, moving lower, until he was sliding his hand into the *V* of her blouse, caressing the sensitive skin just inside the cup of her bra, teasing, only to draw back out and make his way down her clothed body, her nipples aching to feel his touch.

She moved her bottom against the erotic promise of him, a sensuous feeling in itself, and he reared back from the kiss, as if surprised it had gone that far.

That made two of them.

She noticed in passing that it was dark outside the windows, and the plane shook slightly, the universe apparently reflecting the rocking of her world.

His cock was hard beneath her, his breathing uneven.

Would it be so bad of her to forget about her career for once and act on what she really wanted? It wasn't as if she hadn't made bad career decisions along the way. And never had she made a bad career decision for such a hot, pleasurable, and immediate payback.

He swallowed, and she set her mouth lightly along his strong jaw that with the beginning of a beard took him from gypsy to pirate in the space of an afternoon. She licked the dimple at the side of his mouth, making her way back to his lips, and kissed him again, nearly jumping out of his lap when he sucked her tongue.

She pulled back with a laugh. "I think you were underestimating your experience."

"I think you were underestimating biology."

She brought her lips back to his and whispered, "You're getting pretty good at lines."

"The role-playing really helps."

He kissed her this time, grasping her chin and holding her still as his tongue sauntered into her mouth. It was either biology or the scotch, but she was feeling something powerful, that was for sure.

Moving by instinct, her good sense meter turned off apparently, she adjusted her position from sideways to straddling his lap as they kissed, hiking her skirt up around her thighs and regretting that she had worn pantyhose. His erection beneath the crotch of her L'eggs pressed against her, hard and substantial and very, very tempting.

He brought his hands from her waist slowly up to her breasts, taking one solidly in each hand, squeezing, not too hard, not too light, and she groaned, digging her fingers into his silky hair, not at all coarse as she had once imagined it would be, since it was curly.

"What were your mother's criteria?" she asked softly against his lips.

"What?" His eyes were unfocused, his cheeks flushed.

"The sperm donor. What were her criteria for him?"

"Tall. Good eyesight. Good bone structure." He sounded hoarse and disoriented, and he went to kiss her again, but she pulled back a fraction.

"That's it?"

He surged forward, ignoring the question, moving from her breasts to the buttons of her shirt to enable him to get closer. He had gotten the shirt undone and slipped it off her shoulders before she realized it. He pressed his lips to her heated skin, down her neck to the cleavage between her overstrained bra cups, nudging the fabric aside to get at a nipple, licking and then sucking. She groaned and abruptly made up her mind to let herself have this moment, this hot forbidden encounter.

*What the hell?* She had already given up the ghost somewhere along the way from their first kiss.

After climbing off his lap, she stood up to yank her hose down and off, along with her panties, while he watched intensely.

"You do have a condom, don't you?" she asked.

He nodded, reaching into his back pocket and extracting

his wallet, the movement emphasizing his hard-on. Unzipping her skirt and sliding it off so she was bare on the bottom, she leaned forward and unzipped his jeans as well, carefully, very carefully, while he sucked in a breath and took out the condom, flinging his wallet to the floor.

"I'm doing this because you're so fucking hot and I want to," she whispered. "Not because I'm giving in to any pressure because you're my boss and you came right out and asked me to like an idiot."

"I appreciate that." He ripped the condom open while she grasped his hot, pulsing cock, then shoved the boxers down and climbed on top.

"Let me." She took the condom from him and slid it down his length. "Those pilots better not come in here."

"Well, at least one of them has to drive the plane."

The plane lurched.

"Wow. You're big."

"I never, ah, measured when it's uh—"

"Shhh." She sat down on his now-sheathed cock, causing them both to gasp, and Talbot's head fell back to the seat cushion, his eyes closing.

"Nice, eh, Mr. Boss Man? You like that?" She was caught between fantasy and what might be the end of a not-very-illustrious legal career. "You wanted to fuck me when you saw me, didn't you?"

She punctuated her words by sliding up and down his pulsing length, so wet she did it easily.

"When I actually saw you, yes," he gasped as she took him impossibly deep inside her. "I mean, not before when you were in the office because then I was just annoyed, uh, you were doing that thing with your pearls and making me—"

She kissed him, feeling her tongue rub against his, and he convulsively gripped her bottom, in a good way.

Pulling away from his lips, she murmured, "This is so bad. Sleeping with the boss. I'm such a naughty girl."

His blue eyes glittered back at her as she moved her hips slightly in a way that made them both moan, and he wordlessly urged her to repeat the motion, his hands firmly on her cheeks, bringing her forward and then back, again and again.

"Now you're supposed to say 'you *are* a naughty girl,'" she prompted, "and threaten to spank my bare bottom."

"Uh-uh. This is just us now, and you're not the least bit naughty," he said, low and sincere, and she laughed.

"No! You're the stern boss, and I'm the naughty girl who works for you. You're not playing right."

"Mmmm, I'm not playing."

The admission went right through her, stalling her for a second. She shouldn't be, either. She shouldn't be playing with this volatile situation, hooking up with her boss. But he slid a hand up to caress her breast and, mesmerized by the shot of pleasure, she settled back into the rhythm.

"Oh, what the hell? I could die tomorrow, you know?" Her breath came shorter as she rode him.

She came up on her knees, moving faster as he closed his eyes, kissing her neck. She was very close. Bracing her palms on the shoulders of his T-shirt—somewhere along the line he had shrugged off that hideous jacket—she finally got around to reading what it said. *I'm with Stupid.*

She came in an incredible burst of years of pent-up sexuality, and he shuddered against her, pulling her close while they rode it out. In the aftermath, he rubbed her back, and she listened as both their breathing slowed.

His T-shirt slogan really summed it up. *Stupid.* Yep, that was her all right. That had been incredibly stupid.

And she was as good as unemployed.


Sex with Camilla was extremely good. So good that as soon as she climbed off his lap, her absence bothered him, and he had to resist the urge to tug her back. He'd wait, he supposed, until he got another erection, which given how turned on she had made him, should not be very long. So he sat there, replete, as she turned her back and started dressing.

That was too bad. Putting her clothes back on and all. He tugged the used condom off, knotted the end, and tossed it into the waste container.

"Do you have to get dressed?"

"Eventually."

"Now, I mean."

She glanced at the door to the cockpit as the plane took a dip that almost knocked her off her feet. She slapped his hands away as he went to steady her.

"There's still a lot of time left to the flight," he pointed out with a smile.

"Zip up your pants, boss man," she said. "The fantasy's over. Time for real life."

After a second, he did so, sorry she was in such a hurry.

She picked up the discarded pearls, but instead of putting them on again, opened the overhead and stuffed them into a pocket of her computer bag, along with the panty hose she didn't bother to put back on, either.

"This is all your fault," she said, buttoning her shirt. "Well, not all your fault. But mostly your fault."

"What is?"

"Our having sex, which means I won't be able to keep this job."

"Because we had sex?"

"*Hello.* Yes."

"Why?"

"For one thing because this is a public company, and a CEO can't have sex with an underling. I'm sure it's against a million HR policies. But you're not firing me."

"Right. I got that."

"I quit."

"What? Why? I mean, are you sure that's necessary?"

"What else should I do? Just have sex with you whenever you're reminded you need to have it?"

Again, he could spot a trick question. So he said, instead, "I don't want you to quit."

"Because you want to have sex with me?"

"Yes."

She scowled. He'd walked right into that one.

"And I want you around, too. I like you. I think."

"You have a screw loose," she muttered. "But then so do I for what I just did."

"You climaxed, though," he noted. "And call me Mason by the way."

"Yep, *Mason,* I came. But it wasn't worth giving up my job."

"Again, I'm not so sure we need to concede that. When we land, I'll call Marcia."

"You will not!"

"Of course I will. I always do when I touch down after a flight."

"Fine, but you won't tell her about this."

"If I don't, how can I ask her whether it's necessary for you to quit?"

"I don't need her to tell me I have to quit. I know I do. This is so not how this is supposed to go."

"How is it supposed to go?"

She sat down across from him, deflated. "I'm supposed to prove to you what a brilliant legal mind I have, and you're supposed to quickly learn I'm indispensible and give me stock options that will make me rich."

"I could give you stock options."

"And then, maybe, just maybe, after working together a few years when I'm well established and don't have anything to prove—and you learn to dress properly—then, *then* maybe you can discover you're in love with me and ask me to marry you."

"I don't believe in falling in love." The only reference he'd ever heard to it growing up was his mother saying that it was an invention to sell products, and he hadn't seen anything since then that had convinced him otherwise. Not that he was really looking.

"You don't believe in love. Yeah, that's a big shocker there. But that's how it's *supposed* to go. Not you being a, well, like you are and cold-bloodedly saying you want to have sex with me the first day and me drinking one too many scotches because I'm so freaked out about that and then you being so hot with your role-playing and your kissing and your *touching me* that I actually wind up having sex with you *on my first day*."

The drinking one too many scotches bothered him, and he felt duty bound to ask, "Was your judgment impaired?"

"Yes," she snapped, then buried her head in her hands. "No. Not enough to matter. I did it."

"You shouldn't feel so bad about sex," he said softly.

"I don't feel bad about sex."

"Any chance we can have it again?"

"I feel bad about who I had sex with!"

"Well, I could marry you, if you want."

"This just keeps getting better."

"I don't think I'd ever find your, or really any lawyer's, services indispensable because, frankly, lawyers end up complicating every transaction needlessly. But if the other side has one, the rule is you have to too so they can complicate it in a way that's good for you to counter-act the complication the other side's lawyer is busy doing in a way that's good for them."

"What the hell does that mean?"

"It means I can't fix that part of how it's supposed to go. Your legal mind being indispensible and all. But I am free to marry, and now that I think about it, it might be a good idea."

"I don't even want to ask why."

"It would provide for a steady source of sex with someone I'm attracted to."

"You don't know too many married people, do you? But sure, no problem. I'll marry you. As long as I get to draft the pre-nup."

"Okay."

"That was a joke. Get it? I'd draft a pre-nup that said I got half of everything if we divorce at any time. Like a week after the wedding."

"I sense you're not taking my proposal seriously."

"I sense you're not even joking about it, which is why I would never even consider it."

He should be offended by her comment, but he was more busy wondering why he was still interested in talking to Camilla, even after they'd had sex. Why he felt sort of sorry for her that she seemed to feel so bad about the situation.

And why he could remember her name. Every time. Almost from the very beginning.

"Besides," she said with a little smile. "I'm sure Marcia would never agree to you marrying me. What's with you two anyway? She isn't secretly your mother, is she?"

"No. But she was a friend of hers. Her only friend probably."

"Is she still alive?"

"Marcia? As far as I know."

Camilla swiped him lightly on the arm. "Don't be a smart ass."

And he realized with a shock that he had been. A smart ass. He had been joking. He smiled, startled at the observation.

"Answer the question. Is your mother still alive?"

"Yes."

"Do you see her much?"

"No. Not much." Or at all really. After he got her out of his company, his mother's bafflement at how Mason had turned out led to a permanent estrangement, except for the monthly checks Marcia sent on his behalf. He almost felt closer to his sperm donor, whoever the hell he had been.

"What about your parents?" he asked, because he wanted

to know. Like joking, it wasn't something he normally did. When was the last time he had wanted to know something about someone that wasn't business related? He wasn't sure.

"My parents? Oh, they're alive. In Detroit. Still bragging to anyone who'll listen that their baby girl went to Harvard. Still hoping I'll get rich off it someday. Still destined to be perennially disappointed."

Those blue eyes looked a little watery, alarming him, and she quickly brought the heel of her hands up to them and pressed hard. "Do you have any aspirin?"

"I don't. I try to limit pain killers as much as possible to keep my brain clear."

"You're a real straight arrow, aren't you, Mason? Other than that hitting on the new girl thing."

"I'm sorry about that," he said. And for the first time he was. Her distress at letting their play progress into full-blown, incredibly hot, not-to-be-forgotten sex made him regret how shamelessly he had wanted it. How willing he was to let the scotch or the natural chemistry they shared, biology, whatever, overcome what she clearly thought was a line that shouldn't be crossed. "Listen, Camilla—"

The plane took a huge jolt from side to side, and he caught her automatically in his arms as she lurched forward. Bringing them both back to sit on his side of the plane, they looked to the cockpit door, which was still closed. Another lurch of the plane, though, and they both automatically turned to the window to see what was going on outside. They had flown above the storm when they first took off, but it seemed as if it had caught up to them. It was dark, with no longer even a hint of sun, and the rain pelted against the wing of the plane in long, hard slashes. A flash or two of lightning followed by thunder made them jump.

"Was it doing this when we were having sex?" she asked.

"I don't know," he admitted. "I wasn't noticing anything but being inside you."

"Such a romantic. First a proposal and now poetry."

He smiled. "You're teasing me, aren't you?"

"I guess, but if you have to ask, I'm not doing it very well."

He tugged her closer. "You're doing it extremely well. I don't even recognize it if other people do it."

"Maybe nobody else ever has."

"That's possible," he conceded.

The cockpit door opened with another sideways dive of the plane, and one of the pilots staggered out, holding on to a strap on the wall to keep upright. "We're having some issues, Mr. Talbot," he called out to them.

"What's wrong?"

"The storm is rougher than we thought and caught up to us a lot faster than we anticipated, so it's still at full strength," he shouted over the sound of it. "The wind speed, the lack of visibility from the rain… We can't fly in this much longer."

"Should we turn back to New York?"

"No, we'd never make it. We're too far out to try it by now. We'll have to land."

Camilla peered outside anxiously, but it was too dark to see anything below. "Land?" she squealed. "Where?"

"If we go sharply north," he explained, again in a shout, "we'll hit Nova Scotia. Halifax is our best bet, and we might just make it."

"Might?" she said faintly to Mason.

Mason nodded at the pilot, though it wasn't like they were asking him for his permission or anything. In this kind of situation, it certainly didn't matter a whole lot who owned the plane.

"Strap yourselves in," the pilot yelled, "and if we have to crash land, put your heads between your knees."

"I was just thinking of doing that," Mason said. The pilot made his way back to the cockpit. "But in a remarkably more enjoyable context."

She looked at him, her lips thinned and her hands shaking as she tucked a stray lock of hair behind an ear. Her cream complexion had made it to paper white by now as the plane turned perceptibly left, and without a thought, he pulled her closer, securing her seatbelt as he did so and then seeing to his own.

The cacophony of the storm permeated the cabin, and he wondered at how he had not heard anything of what was going on outside until now. Too engrossed on what was going on inside.

And it had been a very enjoyable feeling.

Her breath, rapid and warm, was against his neck as they endured the bumpy ride for a few minutes more until she broke the silence by saying, "When I said I might die tomorrow, I didn't mean, like, literally tomorrow. This job is really turning out to have been a bad career move."

"We'll be fine," he said calmly, even though the two successive bumps right after his pronouncement—as if the plane had hit an air pocket and then lurched on—weren't giving him a lot of confidence on that score. But he did feel calm. Strangely calm. Perhaps the endorphins released in his recent orgasm were contributing to that. Or maybe he was just glad to be here with her.

Clearly, there was something wrong with him.

# Chapter Four

Mason held her hand as the plane shook up and down and pretty much threatened to make her lose her scotch. Her hand was trembling, but his, which felt steady and warm against hers, wasn't.

Was this sudden turn of events all some kind of wildly out-of-proportion punishment for her lapse in professional judgment? Christ, she'd thought disbarment was the worst they could do to her for failing her lawyerly duties. Who said anything about plane crashes? She was clearly having a terrible, horrible, no good, very bad day. She should have listened to Shreeman after all.

Oddly enough, though, the looming danger had an effect on Talbot, too. It rendered him unusually composed and reassuring. When he put his arm around her and buckled her up, and even when he nodded at the pilot, he seemed more like a CEO than he ever had before then. She liked this strong, controlled side of him. Maybe life-and-death situations did that for the guy.

Or maybe it was the sex.

Whatever, she clung to him, not ashamed to be the obvious wimp that she was. Burying her head in his shoulder, she said the first thing she could think of. "Have you ever been in a plane crash before?"

"No." He brushed her hair out of her eyes. "Which is a shame, since statistically speaking, if I had been, it would be unlikely that we'd crash now. As you might imagine, the chances of one person being in two plane crashes, where flying is not their job, of course, is slight at best."

"There's a flaw in that logic somewhere," she muttered.

"Don't think about it too hard."

"What? Crashing?"

He brought his face very close to hers, brushing his lips against her temple. "Anything."

She shook her head. "At least this is putting my ruined career in perspective."

"I am sorry if I ruined your career."

"No, you didn't. Well, you did a little. I did the rest, I guess."

The plane took a precipitous dive that snatched any further words right out of her mouth. When they stabilized, sort of, she babbled on to keep the thoughts out of her head. "You're really kind of nice."

He pulled back a little to look at her. "I am? Does that mean you'll marry me?"

"No!" She laughed. "You're insane! Though maybe that *is* how this is supposed to go. We're supposed to realize we're meant to be together right before we plunge to our fiery deaths."

"I think it'd be our watery deaths if we don't make it to Nova Scotia."

"Thanks so much for that clarification."

"But let's not keep thinking about how it's supposed to go. Okay? Let's just let it go how it goes."

"I'm scared," she said abruptly. "I'm scared I'm going to die, and I haven't done anything but work."

He said nothing.

"How about you?" She squeezed his hand. "Aren't you scared?"

"I'm less scared about what happens when we crash than I am about what happens when we don't."

The plane swooped down, lower still, and she let out a terrified yelp. She wasn't embarrassed about it, either.

With the darkness outside the window, it was impossible to tell how high they were or weren't relative to the ground. Or even if it was ground. It could still be water for all they knew.

"What do you mean?" she whispered when she could, huddling even closer to him. "That you're more scared if the plane doesn't crash?"

He kissed the top of her head. "I mean I don't want you to quit."

"That's it? Well, don't worry about it. That's not quite the catastrophic issue I thought it was a half hour ago."

"I want to have sex with you again."

One step forward and two steps back.

"You know you should work on filtering out things before you say them."

"I will."

She wrapped her arms around his waist. "Did you, I

mean, *do* you," she purposely kept it in the present tense, "like your work? Designing and thinking up and making those thingies? If you do it all the time, do you at least like it? I wouldn't have minded the hours I worked if I at least liked it. But I didn't."

"I do. I did. I never minded working all the time. It was all I had. All I wanted." He talked freely, quickly, filling up the horrible time it was going to take to see if they made it. "But now I think something was missing."

"Don't tell me, let me guess. Fulfilling your biological urges on a more regular basis?" She would have thought she was too scared to joke, but apparently not. Gallows humor anyone?

He laughed. "Maybe. Maybe something more. I don't know now."

The plane kept descending, feeling nothing like the countless descents in the air she had felt a hundred times or more. No smooth gradual motion, so slight you had to look out the window to register it. Instead the plane was jerking side to side along with the vertical drops, so hard and disconcerting her teeth would be rattling if she didn't concentrate on keeping her jaw locked.

Her face must have shown the effects of the descent. The pure unadulterated panic she could feel rising in her even as the plane itself dropped.

Mason watched her, urgently, intently. "What would you like to do if you could?" he asked, loud enough to make himself heard over the increasingly deafening rattle of the aircraft and continued fury of Mother Nature.

"Camilla!" he called her attention back. "What did you want to be when you grew up? When you were little?"

She shook her head. "I don't know," she mumbled.

"Tell me," he demanded, keeping her gaze on him with the force of his somehow.

"I think I wanted to be a pilot," she finally said, laughing at the irony of that at this very moment. "I never saw myself as a flight attendant like some little girls did."

"Wimps," he said with a smile.

"Just less full of themselves, I think." She had to shout now too, and keeping the volume up helped to block the rest of it out. At least a little. So she kept it up. "But I was always wanting to run the show. Always the pilot. Not that my big sisters would let me if they were in the game."

"Smart enough to be whatever you wanted to be, I bet."

"Well, dumb enough to think I could be anyway."

"You have sisters?"

"A ton of them."

"What?"

"A lot. Eight kids total."

"Eight? Wow. You're kidding?"

"Would I kid you at a time like this, Mason?"

He was smiling steadily, tugging her closer, keeping eye contact. He really did have the deepest blue eyes. His sperm donor must have been something.

"What was it like growing up with so many kids?"

Answering that could at least take up the rest of the time here. But she couldn't find her usual longwinded, many-faceted response to that inevitable question and just said, "Crowded!"

"What number are you in the birth order?"

She shut her eyes tightly, trying to transport herself out of where she was. To put herself in that big house in Detroit with her six sisters and her little brother. "Seventh. I was seventh. Youngest of seven girls. I had a—I mean *have* a—"

The plane took a bump so hard her luggage tumbled down from the overhead compartment, barely missing them, and the cabinet where she'd gotten her scotch came unlatched from whatever held it to the wall and started careening up and down the aisle, crashing with her carry-on.

Oh God, she could not do this. She thought about something her mother had once said about childbirth, a subject about which the poor woman understandably knew volumes. There's a moment in the delivery room, she had said, where there's all this pain and you have a panicked feeling that you can't get out of it. That you just have to do it.

And then, she had followed up with a beatific smile, you go right through it and everything is okay and they hand you this beautiful baby.

She couldn't die. She just couldn't.

And she had always wanted children, she thought suddenly. She'd never known it, but right now she did. She knew it.

And it was never going to happen.

"Open your eyes, Camilla," Mason barked, shaking her to bring her back to him. "We're going to land. That's all. You have a what? Tell me!"

"A little brother."

She whispered it, but he heard, or else he could read lips.

"One boy and seven girls? Jesus, he must be spoiled."

"He's great. Joey is so great."

And she started to cry.

The wings clipped something solid in terrifying bites as they descended, tipping sharply one way and then the other to avoid it, like a drowning person gasping for air, and the plane came down in one bone-crunching move that keeping her jaw locked had not spared her. Suddenly, they were skidding along whatever surface they were on, going so fast on the ground that if there were even the slightest tree or pole in their path they would surely get their fiery death. Maybe watery would have been better.

And she and Mason held on to each other for dear life, their eyes locked in a desperate closeness as the world shattered around them. They clung to one another as if not a breath should try to come between them, not knowing or caring where one of them began and the other ended. Whether it was advisable or not, whether they would have been better served by cradling their heads low between their knees or reaching for the oxygen masks, which had come down at some point, or whatever, they didn't do any of the things flight attendants had warned them to do in the event of disaster on every single airplane they'd ever been on. Instead they held tightly, fiercely, to each other.

Holding on to each other felt so much more reassuring.

By the time the plane jolted to a stop, hot tears rolled down her cheeks, and the blood coursed through her veins like never before.

She took an impossibly deep breath. The plane had stopped. They were alive.

The cockpit door burst open just as they loosened their hold on each other, and both pilots came out, drenched in sweat and beaming.

"We made it!" one of them said.

"Fucking amazing!" the other one chimed in.

Camilla sat up, away from Mason, wiping the moisture

from her face with her sleeve, feeling disoriented. When he went to unsnap her belt, she brushed his hands away and did it herself. He did the same, still seeming calm and self-possessed, looking over her shoulder. "This doesn't look like Halifax."

When she recovered enough to peer out the window, through the sheets of rain and unnatural darkness that came with a storm rather than nightfall, all she could see were rows of trees, branches whipping around in the wind, so dense in their green that they barely provided a pause in the otherwise black around them.

"We didn't make it to Halifax." The pilots looked out the window of the door to the plane, turning various knobs, pulling back latches. "We were flying blind, the fuel gage plunged, and we had to land. Thank God, this was here."

They opened the plane door, letting in a gust of rain and wind, and gestured for them to get up. "We better get right out. This jet took a hell of a beating. No telling if there might be a fire that broke out. We'll check around the perimeter, make sure it looks okay and that there are no signs of trouble before we do anything else."

"I understand," he said, reaching for his ugly suit jacket and putting his hand on Camilla's elbow to steer her out before him. Her legs were shaky when she stood.

After losing it on the plane as she had, she shook off Mason's hand, wanting to walk on her own down the stairs, though she had to grip the railing tightly to do so. When she got to the ground, she nearly slipped on the combination of the mud and her still shaky legs, righting herself at the last minute and glaring around to see if anybody caught it.

Only Talbot did, right behind her, watching her closely.

The pilots walked around the plane with flashlights, shielding their eyes from the rain as they examined the engines, talking in tones to each other she could not hear, before one of them said loudly, "Looks all clear."

Camilla tipped her hot face up to the steady fall of the cooling drops as the pilots slapped each other on the back and grinned. She heard Mason in the background saying, "We really appreciate what you did up there."

No etiquette lesson required.

He must need a potential plane crash to behave like a normal human being. Or when it counted, he knew the right things to say. And she hadn't even thanked the pilots for the ultimately safe landing. She would. She absolutely would. As soon as she got herself together.

Cupping her hands to catch the rain, she splashed some on her cheeks and neck, consoling herself that she at least had not wet her pants, if nothing else. Well, she hadn't barfed either she supposed. But other than that, she'd pretty much fallen apart while her boss stayed calm.

It said something about modern intimacy that she was more embarrassed by her weakness and her closeness with Mason during the harrowing plane descent than she was about having sex with him.

And she absolutely hated the crying thing. Anything but that. With seven girls, her parents were tired of tears by the time they got to Camilla, and she never indulged in the exercise of crying, since it did her no good.

She swiped her hands across her face a number of times, sure any traces of makeup were long gone, until she thought she looked as normal as a girl could look after a brush with death and everything, and then she went over to the others.

Starting with the pilots was easy. They were grinning now like little boys at a candy counter, patting the plane as if it was their faithful dog right beside them, and she said, "I can't thank you enough for getting us through that."

In the tough guy way pilots were supposed to do it, they minimized the feat with a lot of "doing our jobs" and so on. She never would have been able to be a pilot now that she thought about it and was surprised that the long ago dream, probably as long ago as kindergarten, had even come up when Mason had pressed her.

He stood quietly by, looking around, and only then did she take in that they were absolutely nowhere, in the middle of a jumble of mud and woods through which the pilots had miraculously detected a strip of land that might have been a runway once but now was far from the carefully laid out and tended pavement she was used to taxiing down and landing on. Crowded with drenched weeds and only just long enough to fit in the descent of their jet without crashing into the trees beyond or the black lake visible to the left, the strip afforded no lights, no painted markers to guide pilots, and most importantly, no traffic control tower or people of any kind manning one.

Mason smiled at her. "See, what did I tell you? We landed safely."

The unreasonable resentment she harbored for the fact that he had stayed calm and she had fallen apart melted away. A flush of gratitude overtook her and she smiled weakly. "Yes, you were right."

She was still shaking, but God, she was alive. They were actually alive.

Whether Camilla realized it, she was still crying. Tears leaked down her face and mixed in with the steady rain as she appeared to be trying to smile. It was nothing like the expression she was always naturally breaking into, even occasionally when she was angry with him on the plane, as if she couldn't help herself. This expression involved only a tremulous stretching of her beautiful pink lips, an effort to smile, not a smile in itself. He felt tender toward her, protective, and at the same time proud of her brave effort to buck up, to shake off the near death experience and try to reclaim her feisty norm. Whatever fears and apprehensions he had—where the hell were they anyway?—melted away, and a surge of exhilaration coursed through him. They had made it, all in one piece, and they were here, now, *together*.

He put his arm around her shoulders, and this time she didn't push him away, shivering. In the exultation, none of them had paid much attention to the fact they were all getting soaking wet.

One of the pilots shown a flashlight down the strip, in the direction they had come from in their landing. "I'm going to go see if there's a sign or building or something we didn't make out."

He headed that way.

"Come on," Mason said to Camilla. "Let's go back inside for a minute where it's dry." He turned to the remaining pilot. "Okay to go sit back in the plane, while we figure out what to do here?"

"Hang on a minute, sir, until the captain comes back. We

want to make sure she doesn't blow."

"What?" she cried in alarm, her fingers clutching at Mason's jacket, as all three of them moved farther back from the plane at the possibility.

"We don't think it will," the pilot added hastily. "The wings were roughed up a little from the tree tops as we came down, but the gas tanks weren't punctured, and there was no sign of leaking fuel, so it looks like the readings must have been faulty. And of course no fires broke out. She's shaken, but she's okay."

He could have been talking about Camilla on that last one.

Mason hugged her closer to him.

"I'd just rather check with the captain," the pilot said, "before we get back in. And if there's some other shelter around here, it might be better to, ah… But if not, we'll go back on board."

"Fine. We understand." Mason surveyed the view in the distance, the captain no longer visible, black closing in beyond the lights of the plane, slashes of rain all around them, and certainly no buildings that he could see. Just woods and a lake and the long gravelly strip they had landed on, a makeshift runway perhaps for air deliveries to wherever the hell they were. Or it had once been. Now there was nothing. He shook his head and shivered a little in the cold air. It was a fucking miracle they were alive.

She stared at him intently as the captain came back, shaking his head. "Nothing but a battered old sign with some kind of word on it I didn't recognize, Indian maybe, and the remains of a shed, a hangar I guess, but I didn't see anything of further use in it. No radio or anything." He waved a folded sheet of something. "There was a map of Nova Scotia, though, so we can take a look at this."

"Okay to go back into the plane?" the other pilot asked him.

"Yeah. Let's do that," the captain answered.

"It's safe?" she said. "It won't blow up?"

"No, it should be fine." The pilots stepped back into the plane, but when Mason tried to urge Camilla, her feet seemed firmly planted on the ground.

"If it was going to blow up," he assured her, "it would have already done it by now. Probably on descent."

He managed to shepherd her back up and into the lit plane, the pilots closing the door behind them, shutting out most of the sound of the rain.

Mason led her to the seats they had been in for the landing, then grabbed a blanket that had tumbled out of the overhead and draped it over her shoulders as they sat down, side by side. He held her hand, which was ice cube cold. "Rest a minute. Just take a deep breath. Do you want a glass of water?"

"I'm fine. I'm good." Her voice sounded stronger, and she bent her head into the crook of his arm, then laughed, a sound that started out kind of off, but ended more naturally, in pure unadulterated...well, something.

One of the pilots, shit he could not remember either of their names, but he thought it was the captain, spread the map against an overhead as they consulted it, conversing in low tones.

"Where are we?" he asked.

"Well, since the radio went out along the way and some of the instruments failed, we can't tell *exactly* where we are," one of them said while the other nodded. "But that sign out there was a help after all. It looks like we landed considerably south of Halifax, in a state park called," he paused and read from the map, "Kejimkujik. That's what was on the sign. This must have been some kind of a landing strip for supplies, undoubtedly planes a lot smaller than this one, so we really lucked out that we made it down safely."

"Luck, hell, Boyd, that was some fancy flying!" His co-pilot slapped him on the back.

"I second that," Mason agreed. "But how far is this *park* from civilization?"

"Says here the total area of the park is about one hundred and fifty six square miles. Unfortunately, we're not exactly sure where we are in it, and with the storm and cloud coverage on the descent, we couldn't see much in terms of nearest cluster of lights, which might've given us some indication of the direction to head."

Mason didn't have much hope, but he pulled out his cell phone.

"No service, sir," a pilot said. "We already checked."

"Right." He slipped it back into his pocket. "I guess we'll have to walk out if you say the radio is down."

"Park itself is in the center of Nova Scotia, but considerably to the west," the other pilot said, tapping the map. "And there's a town to the north, Caladonia. Might make sense for us to split up, two of us go west, the other two go north."

"Nova Scotia's an island province of Canada, right?" Camilla directed her question to the clean-cut, military-looking pilots in their wet white uniform shirts, stripes on their shoulders, with an attention that Mason didn't like for some reason. "Will anyone be searching for us?"

"It's an island, miss, but a big one. And couldn't say if anyone's looking for us yet. With the radio out, we couldn't send a message that we intended to change course. For all we know, the last airport that was tracking us won't even have picked up the distress signal. And the airport we were originally heading to, Heathrow, won't notice until we fail to show up at arrival time. By then, everybody might think we went down."

Camilla shivered. "My family."

She must be troubled about a call going to her parents, all those siblings, the worry she would be putting them through.

All he had to be concerned about was Marcia. And hell, she wouldn't worry. She'd just mount an all-out search for the plane, convinced she could rescue him wherever he was, even if that was three miles down in the depths of the ocean. He smiled. She probably could, too.

"We might run into a ranger's station, even before a town, where we could get a message through that we're safe," Mason suggested. "Maybe even before they know we're missing."

"God, I hope so," she said in a small voice.

A pilot went to one of the closets and pulled out two leather jackets, trimmed with sheep's fleece, throwing one to his co-pilot as they both shrugged into them. "I would suggest Ray go with one of you, and I'll go with the other."

Camilla nodded, waiting for Mason to get up so she could get by and they could pair off.

"Okay. I'm all for walking out of here," she said.

Mason looked down at her spikey heels. "Not in those shoes, you're not." He turned to the pilots. "Maybe she should wait with the plane, in case someone spots it."

"I don't want to sit here all alone." She glared at him. "I

have flats in my bag."

"It could be a long walk, miss, and in this rain there'll be a lot of mud. We trained for this kind of thing in the Air Force. You let us handle it."

"Right. These men trained for this, Camilla. Let them do their jobs. You stay here in case someone locates the plane. And whoever gets somewhere first will send help back, and if instead someone finds the plane, you can get help to us. How's that?"

She clenched her jaw and shook her head.

The pilots opened the metal container of edible supplies, passing up the drawer with the small bottles of liquor for the one with water and energy drinks. They filled two backpacks, adding some trail mix and other snacks, not weighing in further as to whether Camilla should be joining one of them or not. From a closet they retrieved boots. "What size are you, Mr. Talbot?"

"Twelve," he answered. "Now listen, Camilla, what if someone comes upon the empty plane? They'll think we're all dead. Then what kind of message will get to your family?"

"Without bodies, they will not. They'll think we did what we did, which was walk to civilization. They'll probably even see our tracks from the plane heading out."

"Not in this rain they won't. The mud will wash the tracks away. And bodies can be flung a great distance from a crash, for your information."

"Too bad," a pilot said. "We have an extra pair but it's a size nine. And Ray and I are tens, so you couldn't use ours."

"I'm fine," he said, glancing at his sneakers.

"Maybe you should stay, too," suggested the other guy— in his defense, they looked very similar in their crew cuts and uniforms and now the bomber jackets.

Mason stood up in the aisle. "No, I'm going."

"Then I'm going, too," Camilla insisted, pushing him out of the way so she could get to the overhead.

"She can go with the captain," the man who'd made the suggestion he stay said. "And you can come with me, sir. Boyd will take good care of her, won't you?"

"Sure. The terrain won't be too difficult, I suspect. Just the hike could be quite a few miles."

When Camilla peeked in the overhead, it was empty, and upon spying her luggage perched on a seat farther back down the aisle where it tumbled, she went down to it and scooted low to unzip the side.

He made up his mind. "Miss Anderson and I will go together. West, or north, whichever you think, and you two head in the other direction."

The pilots traded a look that said they didn't want to interfere with the boss and shrugged. One went to the cockpit and came back with two small rectangular black instruments, handing one to Mason and keeping the other.

"Walkie-talkies. They have a range of fifty miles, so at least we'll be able to be in contact if we need to be for that distance, and hopefully, one of us will get somewhere before then. If you have any problems or questions, just depress the button and contact us." He added in a lower voice, "Map indicated there's a fair amount of wildlife on this kind of preserve. Moose, and, ah," he lowered his voice even more, "black bear occasionally."

Mason glanced back to Camilla, who either hadn't heard or was pretending she hadn't. He took the walkie-talkie. "I'll give it another try in keeping her here on the plane. Maybe

I'll have more luck after you guys leave."

The pilot glanced over his shoulder. "She does look pretty wired, and it's going to be a long haul."

He nodded.

"If you do change her mind, just get us on this, and one of us will start heading in the other direction. You could stay on the plane with her."

"No, I'm going."

The pilot handed him the backpack. "Let us know anyway, and if we're not too far, one of us will double back and join you."

"Thanks. But I don't know that'll be necessary."

"Whatever you say, sir. There's an extra jacket in the closet, but not one for her I'm afraid."

"She can have it."

"Two umbrellas in the backpack."

With a final good-bye called down to Camilla, the pilots left after confirming they would go west and handing a compass to Mason that they should use to head north.

When they were alone, the sound of the pilots receding, he closed the plane door against the rain. She tried to pass him in the aisle, suitcase behind her, and he caught her arm. "You sure you're okay?" he asked.

"Am I okay?" Her voice was filled with wonder. "I'm alive. We're alive!"

He smiled. "I know. Hard to believe. That was a hell of a—"

In the confines of the aisle, their bodies practically brushed against each other, and her face was close enough to kiss. Whatever he had been about to say, it flew right out of his head as every fiber of his being dismissed any plane crash in favor of reliving the interlude that preceded it. Being with her…his mouth on her soft lips, his tongue exploring, his cock thrusting up into her warm depths. He didn't want whatever they had started to end.

He cleared his throat. "I, uh, I should let you by."

But he didn't move.

And neither did she.

She kept her eyes focused on the neckline of his shirt, still clutching the handle to her roll-on suitcase. He concentrated on the delicate shell shape of her ear until he started to imagine tracing its swirls with his tongue, tugging on the lobe gently with his teeth. He moved his eyes to her chin, a safe zone he hoped, but he only found himself wanting to taste that, too, then her neck, every inch of her…

"We, ah, we were lucky." She said it softly, a wisp of breath along the top of his T-shirt.

"Yes." He could barely get the one word out.

"It could have, ah, it could have been a lot worse."

"Hmmm."

She looked up at him just as he was remembering how full and soft her breasts had felt in his hands, how eagerly she had ridden him, and he glanced down to see her nipples poking against the silk of her blouse. He met her gaze as she bit her lip and let go of the suitcase.

"I should really get, ah, undressed— I mean *dressed*! *Dressed*! Ready I mean. To walk out of, ah…"

Her cheeks were flushed, and he bent his head ever so slightly. Her lashes dipped and her chin lifted.

And still there was a breath of air between them, and they both held their hands at their sides, not moving, not reaching out to each other.

"Camilla—"

"Mason—"

With the simultaneous whispers, they closed the distance, both of them at the same time, frantically, wildly. He dug his hands into her hair, cupping her head as their lips came together, their tongues tangling, moans and pants filling each other's mouths.

"I want…" she mumbled, and "I need…" was his response as, still kissing, they fumbled to the end of the aisle and he backed her to a wall, harder than he meant to, but she was just as urgent, unzipping his pants and shoving his briefs down. He ran his mouth along her neck, her nipples through the silk, dampening it as he nipped, and she moaned, taking his throbbing cock in her eager hands and stroking, petting, till he gasped and grabbed her wrist to stop, afraid he'd come in her hand, her touch so sure, so hot. He yanked her skirt up.

The surge of life, of energy, that sparked between them was impossible to resist, and he didn't stop to question it, reaching between her thighs, thanking God that they hadn't crashed and also that she hadn't put her hose back on. He slipped his fingers beneath the crotch of her underwear and found her soft and wet as he rubbed her clit, the heat of her making his bare cock against her thigh throb even more. "Oh, yeah," he mumbled against her lips.

But she had no time for foreplay.

"Rip them off," she panted, adjusting her position to hike her skirt up even higher, and with one quick tug that tore the sides of the flimsy silk, he left her completely and beautifully open to him. He tossed the panties into the aisle, and before he could move away to grab another condom— which he was absolutely going to do if he could manage to stop savoring her warm, wild mouth for a second—she placed his hands on her sweet bare ass and her hands on his shoulders and he was lifting in one swift movement to seat her, slick and hot, on his aching cock.

"Fuck," he moaned.

"Yes…"

His jeans around his knees, he pulled back slowly till the tip of his cock was almost out of her hot clench. Then he slammed into her, hard, again and again, making a slapping sound against the wall, as he grasped the gorgeous cheeks of her ass, her feet still in her heels linking behind him.

"Yes, yes…oh, God, I…"

Her head fell back, the upswept hair more down than up, and he buried his face in the curve of her neck, tasting the sweet moistness there, clinging to her with a fury, her eyes closed, breasts bouncing against his chest beneath the silk of her blouse as he fucked her.

"I should," he tried to get out, maneuvering her desperately so he could go even deeper, grinding his cock into the tight wet clasp of her, "I should really get a…"

"Yes!

"Fuck!"

They came together in a burst of intensity, of pleasure that surely must have mimicked the first time Adam and Eve got it on in the garden and realized how incredibly alive they were.

Now *that* was poetic.

# Chapter Five

"A condom," he whispered when he could breathe again, letting her slide down the wall until she stood. "That was what I was going to say. I should get a condom."

She smiled at him, radiating some kind of crazy joy that made her even more beautiful and conversely rendered him almost shy. She tugged her skirt down and tossed the ripped panties into the trash. "That's okay. I remembered I want children."

"What?" he said in alarm. He wasn't exactly ready to be a father right now. Well, maybe ever. But even that thought couldn't mess with his head right now. He was too sated. Content.

"I'll get my flats and maybe something warmer, and we can get going."

She retrieved her roll-on suitcase and headed to the bathroom. "Just give me a minute." She hesitated. "Now that I think of it, don't you have a suitcase?"

"Didn't need one. I have an apartment in London. I keep clothes there."

"Oh okay." She disappeared into the bathroom.

After a minute or two, still catching his breath—and resolutely ignoring the kids comment—he saw his wallet at the end of the aisle where it must have slid with the jostling of the storm and landing. He'd never retrieved it after they first had sex. He walked over and bent to pick it up. On impulse, he searched around for her computer case, found it under a seat, and opened the side pocket to retrieve her pearls. He slipped them into his jacket pocket right as the door to the bathroom opened. She had pulled on a sweater over her blouse and changed into jeans. Ballet-looking flats that didn't appear to be suited to the rain were in her hand, and she slipped them on to her stocking feet.

"Do you think we'll need ID?" she said, nodding at his wallet that he still held.

He extracted what he was looking for, pleased that Marcia as ever had discreetly made sure he had three condoms in his wallet, so there were two left. Waving them at Camilla, he said, "Just being safe."

Her eyes narrowed and her chin went up. "I was only kidding, what I said about having children."

"No, I didn't mean—"

"I had my period earlier this week. So it wasn't an issue. And as I told you, after one scotch too many, I haven't had sex in forever. So I'm certainly healthy. Don't worry about it."

"I wasn't worried." He slipped the condoms into his jacket pocket alongside the pearls.

"Apparently, you were." Her voice shook a little as she

headed toward the door, and he caught her arm.

She looked up into his eyes, and he was horrified to see that hers were watery. Swiping at them, she bent her head and pulled away. "I'm still shaky from the whole plane thing. Don't mind me. Of course I shouldn't be offended that you reach for your condoms at the prospect of being alone with me. Why wouldn't you? I've jumped you twice now, haven't I?"

He shook his head. "I didn't mean it that way."

"Come on. Let's go."

"Camilla." He forced her to face him, but then wasn't sure what he wanted to say. All he could think of was, "I'm pretty sure I jumped you that last time."

She smiled. "Uh, I guess we jumped each other maybe. I don't know what got into me."

"I think it was the not crashing and dying part."

"Yeah, that might have had something to do with it." Her smile widened.

"I could look at you smile all day," he said softly.

She dipped her head, as if embarrassed.

"Simply an observation." He looked away.

"Hey." She touched his arm. "What do you say, for now, we forget about the, ah, unconventional circumstances and just go with the flow until we get out of this. Whatever happens, happens. We still have a long walk ahead of us. Let's not be awkward with each other. Okay?"

"I'm awkward with everybody."

"You're doing pretty well with me," she said with a twist of her lips.

"Yes, why is that?"

"The not crashing and dying thing?"

He shrugged, reaching for the bomber jacket from the closet. "Here."

"No, you wear it. I have this sweater."

"I'm strapping you to the seat unless you put this on. It's too small for me anyway, and I have my suit jacket."

"Oh, all right. Thank you."

He handed her an umbrella from the backpack the pilots had filled with water and snacks and she opened the plane door, starting down the stairs without him and striding off into the darkness. He retrieved his own umbrella, slugged the backpack over his shoulder, tying the laces of the size nine boots together and slinging them over his shoulder as well, and hurried out to catch up with her, flicking on his phone flashlight on the way. The rain splashed around their feet and beat against the top of the umbrellas as they walked in the direction the compass claimed was north. Her ballet slipper shoes were half submerged in water but she kept pace as if they were wellies.

A half hour of mud later, she resorted to the boots, wadding her socks up in the toes so they wouldn't fall off and double-tying the laces.

The trail they eventually wound up on appeared to be abandoned, overgrown with nature taking back what had once been her own in the first place. They had to take care, flashing the light to make sure they didn't trip on stray roots or rocks. That, along with the still deafening sound of the storm, precluded conversation as they set a dogged pace. After a while, the rain eased off, but the sky darkened into true night. Periodically, Mason shone the light around them on their environs to try to make sure they weren't missing a sign or other evidence of people, but for the first few hours, there was nothing.

Beside him, Camilla hugged the oversized jacket to her slight frame, umbrella perched on her shoulder, and when the rain lightened, she collapsed it and walked in what was no more than a heavy mist. A sudden downpour a few minutes later had him struggling to shield her with his umbrella as she reopened her own, not fast enough to avoid getting so wet that her blond hair looked as dark as his and her jeans were soaking.

He shook his head. They couldn't keep this up all night. But he didn't say it out loud.

The walkie-talkie sounded up just once, a few hours into their journey with a brisk, "Anything in sight, Mr. Talbot?"

He stated there wasn't and received a similar report on the other end.

Camilla, under an umbrella again, walked ahead of him even faster.

Later, just as he was about to insist she stop and rest, at least drink some water or something, she snapped her attention to the right and said, "What's that?"

He shone the light in that direction to see a one story, tin-plated building, flat roofed and square but more than good enough for some temporary shelter. Off the trail a hundred feet or so, the dilapidated condition of the building exterior, rusted and gaping out in places, suggested it was not in frequent use, whatever it was.

He rattled the padlock on the front door, a faded black lettered sign announcing it was Luxton Lake, Station S-5, whatever that meant.

Although the building was locked, it sported a row of evenly spaced ground floor windows in the front, none of which were barred or boarded up. Mason broke one easily with the handle of his umbrella and reached in to open the metal latch. Once open, he hoisted her up and in.

"I hope it's a garage with a jeep full of gas." She landed with a slight jump, and he climbed in after her.

They looked around. It wasn't. Just a big utilitarian-looking room with a wooden table and chairs, one rusted sink, a battered locker, and an unlit fireplace.

And a bed.

"Even better," he said. "We need to rest."

The bed was stripped of sheets or blankets with a thin used-to-be-white mattress gracing a metal frame. She opened the locker, but its shelves were empty. When he turned on the faucet, only a cloud of dust emerged from the spout.

"Nothing here." Her voice was quiet in the room, no echoes from the cement walls and floor.

"I wouldn't say that." He sat on the edge of the bed, patting next to him. "You look tired."

"Shouldn't we get going?"

"First let's rest."

She shook her head, but smiled slightly. "Condoms burning a hole in your pocket? What happened to my clueless boss?"

He hadn't been thinking of the condoms.

Not exactly.

But now that she mentioned them. "He's catching on?"

She paused. "Or he was there all along."

He leaned back on his palms. "You're not still talking about that movie with the limp-dicked guy tricking Madonna or somebody, are you?"

"Marilyn Monroe. And I'm surprised you know who

Madonna is."

"Me, too, but it's kind of unavoidable."

He shrugged out of his jacket and spread it to cover part of the mattress. Unfortunately, she looked around, everywhere but at the bed, her lips thinned, arms crossed. "Sometimes you sound so stiff and unapproachable, and then other times you sound just like a regular guy."

"I'm nuanced," he said.

She laughed. "And to answer your question, no I'm not still thinking of *Some Like it Hot*."

"Okay, because I wasn't about to whip out the condoms, either. I just meant rest. You look beat."

She eyed him.

"Although it's nice to know they're there, isn't it? In case you want to jump me again."

She laughed. "No comment. For now, I guess that ship has sailed anyway."

"What ship?"

"Stop that." But she smiled.

"I'm not presuming anything, Camilla. Just, ah, you do need to rest. Or maybe I do. You're making a wimp out of me with your pace." He tugged at her hand. "Now your feet are soaking wet, and we've been walking straight for three hours. This might be the only dry place we can stop. Come on, we can share a bag of Cheez-Its."

"Actually, I *am* starving." She went over to the table and blew at the dust, then crouched before the fireplace, bereft of wood. "Do you think whoever's in charge of this place would mind if we sacrificed one of those chairs in the interests of trying to warm up? All the wood outside will be too wet to help us."

He stood. "I can handle the chair destruction if you can find some matches."

"Matches? You wound me. I was almost a Camp Fire Girl."

"Almost? I'm impressed." One of the rickety old chairs transformed into kindling with a few firm whacks of it against the iron sink, and he handed her the remnants of the legs. "They had Camp Fire Girls in Detroit?"

She set to rubbing the sticks and making sparks she could blow on. "Well, not technically, but in the summers we stayed at our cottage in a little town outside of the city called Bunny Run, and my older sisters and I would camp at this part of the lake that was filled with weeds and foliage that hadn't been cut down, and we'd pretend we were Camp Fire Girls. We called it the natural beach because it was a sandy cove, despite all the other guck around it."

The flames started out shimmery and as faint as the flicker of a lighter, but seconds later they managed to spread enough to qualify as a real fire. Mason and Camilla both rubbed their hands together over the warmth, and he dragged the bed over, metal legs scraping against the cement, to right in front of the fireplace.

"What?" he asked at her raised eyebrow. "We need the rest of the furniture for potential kindling."

"Mmmm."

He sat on the bed, leaning back on his palms again, and she stood beside him, holding her hands out to the burgeoning fire before she untied her comical boots, kicking them off, and he did the same with his sneakers, both of them warming their bare toes before the fire.

"What about you? Were you a Boy Scout?"

"I went to boarding school. No Boy Scouts there."

"You did? Oh right, that's some fancy thing they do out east, right? Where'd you go? Andover? I think that's the only one I know the name of."

"You wouldn't have heard of mine. And it wasn't out east. It was in Northern California."

He rarely thought of the sterile halls of St. Fischer's anymore whereas he used to dream of it all the time. And in the dream he was always the same age he was when his mother left him there with the head master and warned him to "be good" with a sigh that told the old man her son rarely was. Or maybe she had just said it outright. He didn't actually remember.

"California? I'm surprised. You don't fit my stereotype of California."

"You should meet my mother."

She cocked her head.

"She's the prototype of the bleached blond, tanned Valley Girl, even at whatever age she is, which she keeps a state secret."

"Huh, must be that sperm donor you got your coloring from."

He watched her frame silhouetted against the fire. "Apparently."

"We all look alike in my family. All blondes. Not bleached," she added quickly. "Just highlighted. Except my parents. Neither of them is blond."

"That's odd."

The damp sweater clung to her and hinted at some of the lush figure he knew was underneath, more than when it was completely dry anyway, but she still had far too many clothes on.

She really should get out of those wet clothes. Just the thought sent a shock of excitement through him.

"Genetics. A lot of recessive genes floating around in the Anderson gene pool." She laughed, retrieving the Cheez-Its from the backpack and breaking them open, taking a handful and offering him one as well. "What grade were you in when you went away to boarding school? High school?"

"No, I was five."

Her head snapped around to look at him. "Five? You're kidding."

He watched the fire leap higher as they finished off the bag of snacks. "You warming up?"

"Yes." She turned around to face him. "I'm feeling all toasty."

"Good." She stood between his legs, and he pulled the bomber jacket off before spreading it below his own on the bed.

"Remember what you said about letting whatever happens, happen?" he whispered.

She took a deep breath. He barely heard her "yes" when she murmured it.

"You have to get out of these wet clothes. Let's do that and see what happens."

Keeping eye contact with her, and slowly enough so she could stop him if she thought the teasing was going too far, he ran his hands along the sides and back of what he was pleased to note were tight jeans, even more so when they were wet.

"You have a beautifully shaped ass." He was so turned on at the prospect of taking his time with her, exploring every inch of her, if she'd let him, that he barely got the words out.

"We shouldn't stay long, Mason. We should be trying to find a town or park ranger or phone or something as fast as we can."

"It won't do us any good to faint from exhaustion on the trail. And it's dark out there. Who knows what we might run across? Better we're dry and well rested, right?"

He pulled her blouse out of the waistband and concentrated on the snap of her jeans, his thumb lodging in her belly button for a second, causing her to jump a little.

"You know what I'm thinking?" he murmured.

"I have a pretty good idea."

"I'm thinking that you could take your wet clothes off while I turn my back and then wrap yourself in the jacket."

One eyebrow went up. "Mmmm, you're surprising me here. That wasn't what I thought you were thinking."

"Or I could *help* you undress, which I really should do."

"And why's that?" She moved a little closer.

"Because I've been inside you twice, and I've never seen you naked."

"It's cold." The protest sounded half hearted.

"Thanks to your campfire skills, it's warming up, though. What else do you have to show me?"

She stared down at him, then said softly, "See for yourself."

He unzipped her jeans then dipped his hand inside to where she was hot and bare.

"Commando," she whispered, and he didn't bother to point out he'd never heard the term. He knew what she meant. "You ripped my panties off. Remember?"

"And you didn't have any others in that suitcase of

yours?"

"Shut up!" She laughed.

He slowly unpeeled her jeans, kissing her silky abdomen as he did so, straying to the light curls at the top of her thighs, darker than her hair but proof positive she was a natural blonde indeed. He left the wet jeans on the floor. "Take your sweater off."

Her breath came faster, and her eyes were a dark blue in the firelight, not light as they usually were. He could see her fighting with herself for a second, and he held his breath, but she pulled the fuzzy pink wool over her head. He slid his palms between her bare legs, widening her stance. "Now your blouse," he whispered, pressing his lips to her puffy clit, which tasted so sweet and tangy. She moaned and when he glanced up, her eyes were closed, her head back. "Go on, Camilla."

She opened her eyes and looked down at him, unbuttoning her blouse quickly. After tossing it away, she used her hands to unclasp her bra without further instruction as he stroked her lightly between her thighs, along her wet core. Then she was naked in front of him in the firelight. There for him to touch and kiss and fuck, her creamy full breasts tipped with dark pink nipples inches from his mouth.

"You, too, now. I want to see you naked," she said in a breathy voice, and he stood, urging her onto her back on the cot.

"Okay." He yanked off his shirt, his pants and briefs gone as quickly, and then reached for a condom in the spread out jacket as she lifted her shoulder to accommodate him. Resting one knee on the bed, he ripped open the condom and rolled it on. "But I'm on top this time."

God, he had been on top from the moment she gave in to his dark blue eyes and black, unruly curls, even wilder from the damp. And as to his talented hands and mouth… How had she ever thought he was clueless? Whatever else her boss may have been oblivious to in life—manners, cultural references, friends and family—he knew his way around women. And she didn't want to think right now about why that was.

She didn't want to feel bad about anything, as she had for those first few minutes after the plane landed, worrying about something that didn't even matter, about who was brave and who wasn't, when all that mattered was that they had survived. She wanted to feel this magic they unexpectedly had together, him moving inside her, kissing her, loving her, making her feel so alive she could not have imagined being so close to death only hours before. She wanted him, no matter how it ended up when they made it back to the real world.

He started to climb on top of her as she lay on the cot, and she sat up, a palm to his chest, halting him. "Not so fast."

He sat back on his haunches, his hard cock rearing up at her, while she smiled and ran her hand lightly along the top of his broad shoulders and down his muscular chest where just a dusting of black hair stretched from each copper nipple and in a thin strip down his flat abs, a perfect six pack. "Now I get to look, too."

Skimming her fingertips from his chest to his narrow hips, the top of his muscular thighs, she said, "How does a guy who works at a desk all the time get such a hot body?"

"Genetics, I guess. Sperm donor, remember?" He sounded hoarse and eager and not content to let her be the only one looking and touching. Whatever pins remained in her hair came tumbling out with his quick fingers tugging down the remnants of the bun. He spread her hair over her shoulders and down her back, where it fell almost to her waist. "Look at you. I didn't know all this was waiting for me." Burying his face in her hair, he cupped her breasts, heavy with wanting him, and she arched against him as he pushed her down again, his hot ready cock burning against her thigh.

Shoving a leg between her knees, he opened her wide, and a sharp pang of pleasure wrenched another moan from her as he brought his mouth to one breast. Her fingers were in his hair as he licked and sucked her sensitive nipples, first one, then the other.

"You taste so good," he murmured against her skin as she arched, his hand between her thighs now, teasing her clit. "And down here, you're so wet. I want to taste you all over."

He moved his mouth lower, to the underside of her breast, her ribs, and then the curve of her hip, warm tingling kisses that she welcomed with breathy hums of encouragement. When he set his mouth between her thighs, she cried out, the black curls silky against her fingers, his mouth hot and insistent. Though she had her eyes closed, she concentrated on the sensation of his finger sliding inside her, the pressure of a second along with the coordinated work of his tongue sending her close to the edge.

"God, how do you do that?" she moaned.

The waves of pleasure intensified as he worked her until she shuddered, clutching his head, the spasms rocking her.

Quickly, he moved up, bracing his hands on the bed, and shoved his hard cock in her so deep they both gasped. A second lunge and her heels came around to his tight buns, gripping him as her arms went around his neck. She held on for dear life as the rhythm he set hurdled her toward another climax before he stopped, hard and throbbing within her.

"Mason?" She opened her eyes slowly to find him above her, his dark eyes hooded, the gypsy curls wild around that beautiful face.

Dropping a light kiss on her mouth, he whispered, "Too fast," and started up again, lazily, teasing her with sure steady thrusts. "I want to savor being inside you this time. I don't want to rush."

She groaned, frustration at being held off before the peak mixing with a deep full satisfaction at how masterfully he kept her there.

"I could fuck you all night," he murmured. "So tight and wet, gripping my cock."

She moaned, using her heels to egg him on, faster, but he ignored her until she leaned up and kissed him, her fingers in his hair, her tongue plunging into his mouth, and he let go of his tight control, slamming into her, cupping her bottom with one hand, getting as close to her as he could until they both exploded, panting, and she fell back on the bed. He collapsed heavily on top of her, their bodies sticky with sweat and their hearts beating so fast against each other's chest she swore she could hear them both.

"God." It was all she could manage to say against his ear, his head in the crook of her shoulder and neck.

"Mmmm." He pushed himself off her and rolled onto his back, his chest still heaving, the narrow bed necessitating that she turn to the side and snuggle into his arms. He dropped a kiss on her temple, smoothing her hair away.

After a minute, she took it all in. Whereas she had ridden him the first time they'd made love on the plane and neither of them had much control the second time, Mason had been in complete charge of this entire performance. From stripping her to going down on her so incredibly well that she actually came from it, not something she was used to on the few occasions old boyfriends had consented to do it, until the coordinated, incredible sex, Mason had been a master.

She lifted her head, suspicious again. "How did you get so good at sex anyway if you supposedly didn't know rich guys could get any girl they wanted?"

He ignored the question, rubbing her back. "I want you."

"No, really. It doesn't…*fit*…with the rest of you. Have you had girlfriends in the past?"

"No."

The answer would not have surprised her earlier, but with her tender bits still throbbing from all his attention, she found it hard to believe. "Why not?"

He urged her head back to his chest, sifting his fingers through her hair. "I've never— It's hard to explain. Why does it matter?"

"Because it does." She heard the drumming of his heart slowing and thought of how he had talked her through the landing. "You were great up there in the plane, too, by the way. Incredible."

He let out an impatient sigh. "I don't know how I got so great at sex, okay? I barely ever have it. And I doubt I am anyway."

"No, you are," she assured him, not bothering to point

out she was talking about the comforting-while-they-were-in-danger-of-crashing, not the sex. He was great at both in any case.

"I don't know how many siblings anyone has," he blurted out.

Way to get her off the subject.

"I never asked anybody that in my whole life. I never cared. I don't even know how many Marcia has, or my mother."

"That's a little hard to believe. About your mother, I mean."

"Not if you knew my mother. I think she makes it a point to stop speaking to anyone she's biologically related to after a fixed timespan and then acts as if they don't exist."

"Wow. That's weird."

"I'm weird." He sighed. "That's what I'm saying, Camilla. So everything doesn't necessarily *fit* with me."

"Well, you've certainly made it work for you, no denying that."

"Camilla," he murmured. "Camilla."

She liked how her name sounded on his tongue in his rough, after-sex voice.

"Like that. I never remember anyone's names. Not even a woman's I've slept with, though I know that sounds harsh. Ever."

"Thought you said you didn't do much of that," she noted, but she was only being snotty now.

"I don't, comparatively speaking. Most of the time, I'm too busy for sex. But sometimes, I'm at some party PR makes me go to, but then sends a suit with me to make sure I leave soon and don't say anything while I'm there. And that's fine.

That's always been fine. You saw me at the meeting in New York. That's how it is at those parties."

"Okay. When do you get to the sex part?"

"There are women there," he stumbled on. "And, well, usually actually, not that I'm at these parties much, but when I am and if I'm thinking about sex which, ah—"

"Get on with it."

"Well, some woman usually comes up to me and asks me to have sex. I know you said nobody's supposed to do that, but I'm pretty sure it's happened to me most of the times I've actually had sex lately. Unless I just, er, suggest it myself, which goes over a lot better than it did with you, by the way."

She neglected to mention to him the billionaire exception to not taking his approach, since it was the corollary to the rich-guys-can-have-whoever-they-want rule. In other words, in the right circumstances, a "*Got sex?*" approach works just fine for both parties; both come out ahead.

"What about before you got rich?"

"I don't remember," he hedged. "I only know I'm sure I've never had sex with the same woman more than once. Other than during the same sexual encounter."

She couldn't help smiling at the clarification.

"Do you really have seven siblings?" he asked.

"Yes, but I don't want to talk about my family right now. I don't want to think about them worrying about me." Speaking of which. "We should get going." She started to sit up and he pushed her down, coming on top of her.

"Not yet. Rest a little more."

His cock, which had softened after sex, started to stretch and harden against her bare thigh.

"I don't think rest is what you have in mind."

He kissed her neck. "I'll be good. I promise."

"That's what I'm afraid of."

But her lids felt so heavy, and he rolled onto his back again, the circle of his arms around her so warm and comforting she forgot they were in the middle of the woods and had to walk their way out. He ran his fingers through her hair slowly. "Rest for a little bit, Camilla."

She lay next to him, humming softly.

She came awake slowly, not sure how long she had been out. The fire was still going, but Mason wasn't beside her. Was that what had awoken her? He stood at the window, still naked, his back to her, and the sight of his lean muscles and firm ass awoke something in her that she thought he had already completely, wonderfully satisfied into near numbness. But the warmth between her thighs, her nipples hardening, proved she wasn't above being greedy.

She stretched and he turned around, semi-erect, which made her smile. He smiled back at her, glancing down with a rueful shake of his head. "I was trying to let you sleep, but having you naked beside me was more than I could take, I'm afraid."

He came over and sat on the edge of the bed, one hand resting casually on her hip.

"How long was I out?" she asked, still feeling sleepy.

"Not long enough." He urged her down. "You should rest a little bit more before we get started again. At this point, we should just wait till it's dawn." After retrieving the bomber jacket, he spread it on top of her, the soft sheep's wool side of it down. It felt wonderfully cozy. "Were you cold?" he asked.

"A little." She would just close her eyes for a second, since her legs still ached from all that walking and her bones felt tired. But then they had to get going. "Shouldn't you rest, too?" she murmured.

Though she could barely hear it, she could feel the laughter rumbling through him as he leaned closer with a light kiss along her neck. "If I lay down next to you, Camilla, sleep is the last thing I'll be getting."

"Mmmm, but you must be tired." Even now, she could feel herself being dragged back down...*into the arms of Morpheus*...until she registered something cold and alien on the mattress underneath her shoulder. She shot up. "What was that?"

He leaned over her to pick it up. "Just your pearls." He dangled the single strand. "I brought them along. They must have come out of my jacket pocket when we were, uh..."

"Yeah. I'm sure they did." She held out her hand. "You didn't need to bring them. They're not an heirloom or anything. I think I bought them at JC Penney."

As she reached for them, he snatched his hand back, keeping the pearls in his fist. "Oh no, you don't. I'm in charge of these now." He nudged her onto her back again, and the bomber jacket fell away as he stretched out, leaning toward her, his hard cock against her thigh.

Her pulse leaped, and she was deliciously wide awake as he let the pearls fall in one looped jumble from his palm.

"Let's see how you like being teased by these for a change."

Her lids drifted closed, concentrating on the light caress of the cool, smooth pearls against her throat, her shoulders.

"You were driving me crazy with these," he whispered as he ran them along the top of her breasts, skimming her nipples slowly only to circle back and do it again.

She held her breath as he rubbed a pearl harder into her nipple, then bent his head to lick the two. His tongue flicked from her to the bead, again and again until she thought she'd cry out from the light erotic play, before he moved on, draping the strand along her stomach, the outsides of her thighs. She bent her legs, opening them slightly in silent invitation, as he threaded the pearls through her pubic hair, a massage of his own fingers and the cool necklace.

"Where should I put these now?"

She could hear the laughter in his voice, and she peeked up to find him on his side beside her, on one elbow, his head propped in his hand as he played with the pearls and her heated body, watching down as he did so. Her breath came faster, excitement building as one lone pearl made it to her clit and he rubbed gently, the slight friction so hot she thought she would jump out of her skin.

"Do you like that?"

She nodded and the pearls dipped lower, slipping into her wetness, the cool surface and his hot fingers working the smoothness against her, with her, teasing and then pushing farther. When she felt him nudge the pearls slightly inside her, she moaned, and he leaned over to place his warm mouth on her nipple, pushing farther inside with the pearls, as he licked and sucked her breasts and she shuddered under his dual attentions.

Jiggling the pearls below, in and out and against her

heated flesh, he moved up to her mouth, a long thorough tasting of her, whispering, "Every time you touched those pearls, this is what I imagined."

She cried out as he went deeper with his play, relishing the novel feel of his fingers working the rounded beads inside her, against her hot, wet pounding flesh, and then pulling them out to rub slick against the insides of her thighs, the tip of her clit, only to shove them between her legs again and again.

By the time she came, she was panting, thrashing her head from side to side, begging for release, and he was murmuring, "Okay, no more teasing," and pulling the pearls out to drape them on her clit, her hips. He ripped open another condom, rolled it on, and in one smooth movement buried himself inside her.

"Oh, God, that feels so good," she muttered as he began a hard, driving rhythm that took them both to the top.

She came down to the feel of the pearls draped over her chest as he took her into his arms, rubbing her shoulders, her back. The exhaustion of the lovemaking and the plane crash and the walk in the mud and rain all jumbled together and culminated in one reverent humble moment of gratitude. She was alive and it was mind-bogglingly wonderful. She drifted into a heavy sleep, swearing it would only be for a few minutes, as they snuggled together, the fleece-lined jacket over them as a blanket.

# Chapter Six

When pink light filtered through the window they'd broken to get in, Camilla surged up, registering that the fire was reduced to ashes. The cold nip in the air shocked her. They'd slept too long. Much, much too long. She prayed the pilots had gotten to a phone and someone had already told her parents they were okay, if they even knew about the crash in the first place.

"Mason." His face in repose evidenced none of the shadows or tension it sometimes did when awake. Firm mouth, with the sensuous lower lip, was only slightly open. Black lashes dusted his cheeks, so long she had to resist the impulse to graze them with her fingers just to feel again how soft they were. "Mason." She shook his shoulder, and he opened his eyes, coming awake all at once, staring at her.

"We have to get going."

His eyes shifted into a darker blue. She ignored the reaction of his cock farther down, which came to attention right away, and stumbled out of bed. "We slept way too long."

Her jeans, which had spent the night in front of the fire, were dry, and she shrugged into them and the rest of her clothes before Mason managed to sit up, elbows on his legs, head bent and hands in his hair as if trying to rouse himself.

No need for any rousing in the lower part of his body. To his credit he didn't reach for her, understanding her haste, though he did glance up with an ironic smile. "You couldn't have put your clothes on before you woke me?"

She tossed him his pants. "Really. I'm so worried we get somewhere so my parents know I'm okay."

He stood and stretched, and she ignored how hot he was in all his nakedness. At least the evidence of her reaction to him was hidden under her layers of clothes now. He pulled his shirt on first, turning away from her, pausing for a minute, rubbing his forehead.

"Come on. What are you doing?"

"I'm conjugating Greek verbs to keep from getting down on my knees and begging you to suck me off."

She laughed despite herself, shocked and, well hell, a little turned on.

He peeked back at her over his shoulder. "I'd be quick."

She shook her head. "I'm sorry. My heart wouldn't be in it right now."

"Would your mouth?"

"Mason!"

"I'm kidding. Just kidding."

He reached for his pants, and she tied the clunky boots on and then got two bags of trail mix out of the backpack. When he was dressed, she tossed him one. "For the road. Now will you wear the leather jacket today? It's only fair. I wore it yesterday. You were probably freezing."

"But I'd still be freezing if you hadn't made the fire. So you deserve it." He wrapped it around her, dropping a kiss on her lips.

He shrugged into his own jacket, pocketing the pearls.

"Am I ever getting those back?"

"Don't count on it. Okay, Miss Anderson, let's get going."

As they headed out, she remembered the walkie-talkie in the backpack and said, "Wait a second," indicating he should turn around so she could extract it. "We should try this. See where Ray and Boyd are."

"How do you remember their names?"

"You should try mnemonics. It might help."

"Marcia's done her best. Believe me. I'm hopeless."

She grinned at him. "You just don't care."

"I care when I want to, *Camilla.*"

"I'm honored." She fiddled with the device. "I don't know why we didn't try this last night."

"We had other things on our mind."

"Hmmm." She depressed the talk button. "Boyd? Ray?" She waited a minute. Nothing. "Guys? Are you there?"

Two more tries proved just as fruitless.

"Come on," he suggested. "Keep it out and we can try as we walk."

All traces of the storm had disappeared, except for the relentless mud. Bright autumn sunshine guided their way through the woods, and an hour or so into their brisk hike, they even found a trail that appeared to be well-kept—still dirt, well, mud really, but a path with no weeds and an occasional sign not to litter. The jacket was too warm to wear after a while, and Camilla tied it around her waist until Mason insisted on stuffing it into the backpack.

Although the walkie-talkie continued to fail to raise the pilots every time she tried, Camilla was starting to feel some hope.

They talked casually as they made their way, never feeling they had to, but as things occurred to them.

Once, as they walked, she glanced at him sideways and muttered, "*Suck me off!*"

Not breaking pace, he responded, "Was that a request? I'd be happy to, but you're in such a big hurry today I didn't dare suggest it."

"No, I'm talking about how you referred to it this morning. 'Suck me off.' I think you're putting me on half the time about what you know and don't know."

"I could have called it fellatio."

"Hmmph. That's what I would have *thought* you would call it. How come you knew that other charming expression for it?"

He laughed. "Believe me, Camilla, when a girl first offers to 'suck you off' and then shows you what she means, and in my case it was for the very first time, it's not a turn of phrase a man could forget. Some aspects of popular culture or slang are simply unforgettable."

She scowled at him, but he clasped his hand in hers and brought it to his lips, and the courtly gesture went a long way toward making her feel better.

If it weren't for the whole "lost in the woods and maybe never finding their way out of it" thing, she might have enjoyed this long space of time to talk with Mason.

"So you grew up in California?" she asked at one point when they got going again after having stopped briefly for necessities, out of sight of each other of course, since she never wanted to be that casual with a guy. "Did you have a big house, small house, what?"

"My mother lived in an apartment, in Los Angeles."

"And you went away to live at school during the school year?"

"Yes. And, ah, most of the time in the summers. The facilities were there anyway. They didn't mind the extra tuition for boarding in the summer, too. I liked it better during those months actually."

"Of course you did. No school."

"No other kids."

He bent to pick up a sturdy branch on the side of the trail and held it out to her. "Walking stick?"

She took it. "Sure. Thanks. So where did Marcia fit in? You said she was a friend of your mom's?"

"Friend might be an overstatement. Marcia lived next door to my mother and, ah, tolerated her, I guess you'd say. Which in my mother's case, made Marcia about her best friend."

She shook her head, concentrating on coordinating her movements with the walking stick. "It's so hard to think of someone like you having a mother like that."

"Someone like me? You mean rich?"

"No. I mean sweet."

He stopped dead in his tracks, and she was several strides ahead before she noticed. She looked back.

"What? You are sweet. I know some guys take that as a personal insult, but I didn't mean it like that."

He started up again. "I'm not insulted. I'm, ah, flattered I guess. Nobody's ever called me sweet."

She teased, "Not even Marcia?"

"More like a pain in the ass most of the time."

"She cares for you. I can tell."

He shrugged. "I guess she does."

"And you care for her, too, don't you?"

"I hired her, didn't I?"

"Mason!"

He smiled and they walked along in silence for a while.

As the sun rose to the left of them, Mason diligent in ensuring that they stayed north with the help of the compass, the optimistic sense of the morning faded for Camilla. They walked farther and farther and still met no hikers, heard nothing from Boyd or Ray, and were still nowhere.

"They have to know we're missing by now," she said as they walked side by side, noting yet again how Mason kept perfect pace with her, always keeping up when she felt bursts of speed that qualified, despite her oversized boots, as trots, and then miraculously slowing when she felt depleted. Letting her set the pace.

"If we don't run into something," he assured her, "someone will be along, or else they'll send someone after us."

"Who will?"

"Marcia probably. Or the pilots if they get somewhere first. Don't worry. Are you tired? Do you want to stop to rest?"

The suggestion had her increasing her speed.

"Guess not." He smiled, adjusting his own, right beside her.

"I don't understand why we can't get them on this." She waved the walkie-talkie in frustration. "They can't be fifty miles away from us already."

"They might be if they traveled through the night."

A flush of guilt felt hotter on her face than the potent rays of the sun.

Glancing at her sideways, he laughed.

"It's not funny. I feel horrible."

"Why?"

"Because by now my parents must have heard, and they'll be frantic."

He took her hand and circled her palm with his thumb. "It'll be okay. Think how happy they'll be when they know you're fine."

"They'll kill me!"

He stopped. "What?"

She tugged him along. "It's just an expression. You know, how parents, or your mom I guess for you, get so worried that when they find out it's okay, their first reaction is sometimes to get mad at you? They hug you and then when they find out you had a flat tire on a date, or claim you did, they start in with 'you could have been lying in a ditch somewhere?'"

"No."

"Well, ultimately they go back to hugging you, but the longer they had to worry about you being in a ditch, the longer you have to listen to them about it before they get back to the hugging."

"You weren't on a date. You were in a plane crash. You'd think they'd understand."

His tight tone made her defend them. "They will. Don't get me wrong. I just feel bad about causing all this trouble.

No, that's not right. It *hurts* me to think of them hurting right now."

He shook his head, not saying anything, and she brought up the elephant in the room again. "I know you don't get along with your mom, but surely Marcia will tell her you're missing and she'll be worrying."

"I sincerely doubt that."

"That Marcia will tell her or that she'll worry?"

"Both."

"Hmmm." The woman sounded like a real bitch. She kept her observations to herself, though, her mind wandering back to her own parents. The air was warmer now, the sun full strength and glinting off the turning leaves, an occasional gold and red peeking out from the relentless green.

"Tell me about the one brother," he urged.

"Joey?" She could almost see Joey's blond crew cut and wide smile, his heavy glasses perpetually slipping off his nose. "The best way I could describe Joey is something one of my sister's boyfriends told us once. I think he was Buddhist. He said there are some people who have lived so many lives and gotten so evolved that they have nothing left to learn on Earth. So they can go on to Nirvana."

"Sounds vaguely familiar, but I haven't studied eastern religions."

"The point is that of those people, only a few are so cool, so advanced, that they choose to go back and live one more life, not so they can learn something but so that others can learn something from them. Those people are special."

"So Joey's a Buddhist?"

"No. Joey's special."

She walked faster. Another mile or so of the same and

he insisted on stopping, fishing some snacks out of the back-pack and a bottle of water for them to share as the supply was depleting.

"This is ridiculous," she muttered, sitting on a boulder just off the trail. "How big did they say this park was? One hundred and fifty-six miles? How do we know we weren't at the very south of it? It might take us days to walk it."

He downed another handful of trail mix. "It is what it is."

"How can you be so calm about all this?"

"Didn't you say let what happens, happen?"

A rustling in the nearby trees brought a surge of hope — another hiker maybe who had a more detailed map of the park or something equally useful, like a car parked near-by? — but when no one appeared, it unnerved her.

"Hello?" she called out loudly. "Is someone there?"

The noise continued, moving closer, and Mason moved in front of her. "Shhh," he said.

She looked at him in alarm and whispered, "Why?"

"Stay still," he said softly and picked up her discarded walking stick before raising it.

Her heart beat faster. She had been in such a rush that she hadn't given much thought to the fact that the terrain was wilderness and there might be something scary lurking within it. *Lions and tigers and bears, oh my!*

"Hello!" The walkie-talkie she had been trying on and off sounded loudly, making them both jump. "Are you there?"

The sound came closer, and Mason grabbed the walkie-talkie and held the speaker against his shirt to mute it.

A lumbering shape became visible in the trees as it got nearer, something black, and Mason whispered, "Back away slowly."

"Are you there?" the walkie-talkie sounded again, muffled, projecting into his shirt.

"I'm here," he said into it, low. "Wait a minute."

"Oh! There you are! We got you!"

The sound of a helicopter came faintly from the west, the frantic rustling at the sudden noise driving the hidden shape into full visibility.

*Fuck*! She froze in place as a black bear, smaller than she would have thought, but hey, a fucking *bear* emerged onto the trail.

Mason raised the stick higher. The clamor of the helicopter as it approached got louder and louder, and the wind stirred up by the blades beat against the treetops.

"We see you!" came through the walkie-talkie. Her would-be savior pushed her back farther behind him, trying to face the bear alone, but she resisted.

*It would have to eat them both, goddamit, and would that fucking helicopter land already!*

After what may have been no more than a second, but felt a lot longer, the bear, on all four legs, loped back into the safety of the trees as the helicopter descended and both she and Mason breathed an audible sigh of relief.

He grinned at her as the helicopter landed on the trail in front of them, and Boyd, still in his uniform, considerably the worse for wear, stained and dirty, got out and ran to them.

"Nice timing. You made it to something on the west side of the park, I take it?" Mason asked.

"Sure did. We were getting a little worried about you, actually, because it turns out the distance going north was a lot less than going west, so when you didn't turn up before us—"

"We stopped," Mason said.

"A lot," she added. "On the trail, I mean. I'm afraid we were probably pretty slow due to me. And did you see there was a bear right there? Mason held him off."

Mason shook his head. "I did not. The helicopter did."

"A bear? Was that what that was?" Boyd asked.

"That or an extremely big wolverine," she joked. "But did you call somebody I hope? To make sure people knew we were safe?"

"Sure did. As soon as we got to the ranger's station we called Miss White."

"Good. Good."

"She arranged for the bird. Come on."

They went back to the helicopter, bending to make it under the still whirling blades, and then it took off, another pilot, not Ray, at the controls. Ray was there, though, shaking their hands and giving them headsets so they could communicate.

He picked up a radio transmitter and spoke into it. "Hello, there. I've got good news for you. Your boss and the lady are aboard."

Marcia's voice came over the radio. "Whew! That's a relief! Welcome back! Listen, they're going to take you to a hotel so you can all get some rest."

"My parents?" Camilla asked. "Do they know?"

"I've taken care of everything. We'll talk when you land."

The helicopter traveled east until a short while later buildings and water came into sight. They landed on a helipad next to a small Mounties station and climbed out. A sign in front read Dartmouth, Nova Scotia.

When they got inside, no more than a few desks and uniformed police around, Mason looked at the screen of his cell phone. "I have service now. I'll call Marcia on my cell. Are you going to call your parents?"

She glanced at her phone, also receiving service, and saw no missed voicemails or messages. Maybe they hadn't even learned of the incident. The large handed clock by the Mounties' desks said it was close to three. "I don't want to worry them if they don't actually know. Marcia said she'd taken care of everything, but I'm not sure what she meant by that. Can you ask her if she called them? That's the only way they'd find out, I think, unless they left me a message I didn't answer, which it doesn't look like they did."

She saw a ladies' room. "I'm going to clean up for a minute. You go ahead and speak to her."

Warm water and some paper towels under her armpits did wonders, but there was nothing she could do about her makeup, or lack thereof. She hadn't brought that along in their survival kit of course. She thought about the long trudge through the woods, the bear, the temporary shelter. Mason had been so sweet, so protective...so hot. All she needed to survive as it turned out was her new boss.

Her *lover.*

She put the thought away, not sure how to deal with it just yet, and took care of some other necessary business—toilet paper was a marvelous invention, leaves not half so convenient—and emerged from the rest room a few minutes later.

Mason was over pacing by the window, still on the phone with Marcia.

"Is that all there is?" he asked into it when she was close

enough to hear. "You're sure? Maybe we should go on all the way into Halifax."

A faint smile as he listened and then he said, "I'm just asking. Don't get all huffy. If that's it for tonight, then that's it. Just text me the address so I can plug it into the GPS, and we'll get there…what? Oh, okay I'll tell her."

He hung up and the faint smile became a big one. "You look a lot better," he said.

"Thanks. I feel better."

They stood there awkwardly and he added, "Marcia's got us rooms for the night at the closest hotel so we can all get some rest." He nodded over at the pilots, one of whom was answering his cell. "She's calling them now about that and some other things. Logistics for coordinating with Halifax on getting another jet. We should be on our way tomorrow best-case scenario."

She doubted there was a best-case scenario for her now that it was sinking in that they were back to the real world. She had a lot to think about. And she sure as hell didn't want to get on another plane for five hours. She supposed driving to the UK was out of the question, but it was almost how she felt. She knew she had to get back up on the horse, but was glad she wasn't facing that until she got a good night's rest. If she never had to fly in a plane again for the rest of her life, that would be fine with her. Unfortunately, until they invented teleporting, which probably wouldn't be less fraught with potential danger anyway, that wasn't practical.

Of course she was probably quitting this job anyway. So why bother to go to the UK at all. Screw the two week's notice thing. Could she drive from Nova Scotia, wherever the hell that was, back to the office so maybe she could see it, her actual office, that is, before she had to turn in her resignation and start looking for another job?

She almost forgot. "Oh, what about my parents?"

He frowned and she knew he had neglected to ask Marcia. "She didn't say anything. Oh wait, she did say—"

One of the pilots came up. "There's a van that's going to take us to the hotel if we want to head out front."

"I told Marcia I wanted to rent a car."

"There aren't any car rental places nearby."

Mason glanced around them, as if noticing the limitations of the small station and annoyed somebody hadn't taken care of those problems before now to make his life easier. He looked very much like the man who had gotten into the limousine with her yesterday—pre-occupied, aloof, whiz-kid billionaire—and not the one who had gotten off the plane with her hours later.

"Marcia says you'd have to take the van to a car rental place anyway," the pilot continued, "and at that point it makes more sense to go directly to the hotel. Do you want me to call her back?"

"No. Fine. That's fine. Give us a minute please."

Suddenly, whatever Camilla wanted to say to Mason, and whatever he wanted to say to her, she didn't want either of them to say it here where there was no privacy. They needed to talk this thing out between them when they were alone, without an audience.

"No, that's okay," she interjected. "I'll call Marcia myself when we're on our way and ask her about my parents. Let's just go to the hotel." Until she turned in her resignation, she was still supposed to be on the job.

Walking over to where the other pilot waited, she didn't

look back to see if Mason followed, but he did, and they all got in a big, black van.

His phone rang almost as soon as they were off. He answered it with, "You didn't rent a car." But after a second he said, "I was about to tell her, but she was going to call you anyway." He held the phone out.

She took it.

"Hi, kid. Some first day, huh?"

She rubbed the back of her neck. "An understatement."

"You okay? Mason sounds fine. Better than fine. See, I knew you'd be good for him."

She glanced at Mason, who was watching her. She hoped he hadn't dared to tell his assistant just how good his new lawyer was to him. She would be mortified by the personal disclosure.

"All things considered, I guess I'm okay. Listen, did you talk to my parents? Do they know about the crash?"

"Don't you worry about calling them, hon. I felt duty bound to notify your parents."

"Oh, no! I was worried about that. I hope you called them back and told them I was fine. I'll call them as soon as I get to the hotel. They're probably sick with thinking that I might have crashed."

"Relax! They know you're okay. But there was a whole stretch where we were still trying to make sure. We knew the plane was missing by morning, and though we didn't let it leak to the news, we were trying to narrow down where it went off course. That beacon thingy, when they did whatever they had to do to track it down."

"They must have totally freaked." She didn't know who she was sorrier for. Her parents or Marcia for having to deal with them in that state.

"Yeah, I couldn't quite calm them down at the time, so I did the next best thing."

A Best Western Dartmouth sign beckoned, and the van turned into the drive.

"I arranged for a jet to bring them on site, but the minute I heard you two were safe I let them know you're okay and everything's fine."

"What? On site where?"

They pulled into the unloading space in front of the hotel and climbed out.

"They're right there at the hotel. They arrived at Halifax maybe an hour or so ago, and I had them sent right there. And when I called them just a few minutes ago to say you'd been found and were on your way, well I tell you I almost cried. And your mama was bawling like a baby. That mother of yours is a doll."

"My parents are here?"

"Yep."

No need for the confirmation, since her mom and dad were rushing through the lobby door, enveloping her in a hug so fierce she had to laugh. She could see Joey inside the hotel talking with one of her sisters, not sure at this distance which one, since they all resembled each other.

"I'm okay," she assured her parents. "I'm okay, you guys."

Through the phone she heard Marcia call out, "Let me talk to Mason."

He stood beside her, watching the affectionate familial display in sort of the same way he'd looked at the black bear, eyes wide, frozen, and she handed him the phone as her mother took her cheeks in hand, staring into her eyes. "Are you really fine? You're not hurt? My God! When Miss White called, we were petrified."

Her father put his arm around her shoulders and kissed the top of her head, teasing, "Don't you ever put us through that again, young lady."

"I'll do my best."

Despite the awkwardness of the situation, it was understandable they would show up. Marcia probably really had *not* been able to keep them away, and Camilla was glad, as ever, to see them. Some of the life-and-death patina of the last day had slipped away, but not so much that she didn't remember how lucky she was to have survived, to have family like this.

The pilots, easily identifiable by their uniforms, no matter how dirty, were ambling into the lobby, and her dad followed them, calling out, "Hang on there. Are you the two who landed that plane?"

"Yes, sir," Boyd said. Or maybe it was Ray. She'd lost track.

Her dad clapped each of them on the back and shook their hands. "I just want to say you have a fan for life. Delivering our Cammy safely out of that storm. My God, words don't even express how thankful her mother and I are."

The pilots accepted the thanks with more of the "just doing their jobs" talk and finally managed to extract themselves to move on to check in as they all entered the lobby. Her mom clutched Camilla as tightly as if they were both still on that plane and in the middle of a crash landing and led her to one of the leather sofas in front of a stone fireplace.

Mason stood off to the side, hands in pockets, examining

the lobby tile, not joining them, not checking in, though he was off the phone.

Her dad went over to him. "And are you the boss, young man? Because I want to thank you, too, for getting us here and for taking care of our girl."

They shook hands as Camilla gently pulled away from her mother to get up and introduce Mason, but never got there. Joey and her sister, it was Brandy, came over with big hugs for her.

"I thought we'd let Mom and Dad have a private moment with you first, but we're so relieved, Camilla." Brandy kissed her cheek as Joey hovered. "My God! What a story you'll have to tell."

Not all of it unfortunately, at least not in front of her protective parents.

"It was something," she said. "And Joey! Aren't you going to give me a hug?"

"I was waiting, Cammy, because Brandy said we had to."

He held his arms wide to her, and she went into them, giving her tall, stocky brother the vigorous hug he always demanded, almost tearing up again at the sight of his sweet face, a grown man's face that behind his black-rimmed glasses had the most beautiful wide eyes and underneath it all the most pure heart. The heart of a child. In some ways, most ways really, the mind of a child. Such a special child. A special man.

"I was so worried, Cammy, because Mom said you were on a plane, and it got in a storm, and maybe you were scared, so we all wanted to come and give you hugs so you won't be scared."

"I'm not scared anymore, Joey."

"Because we came?" he asked.

She glanced over to where her parents appeared to be trying to make conversation with Mason, who was staring at her. Staring at Joey.

"Yes." She patted her brother on the shoulder. "And now you get to stay at a hotel!"

Brandy took Joey's hand and said, "Let's go to that gift shop over there and get a cookie."

His face lit up, and Brandy led him away.

Camilla hurried over to where her mother and father were in front of Mason. "Mom, Dad, looks like I missed the introductions, but this is Mason Talbot, my boss. Mason, my parents, Jack and Ann Anderson."

"We were just saying to Mr. Talbot what a good lawyer you are and how lucky he is to have you."

"Dad!"

He laughed and hugged her shoulders tight, then loose as they faced Mason. "I'm just kidding, sweetie. We were asking Mr. Talbot if he arranges such an exciting first day for all his employees."

"And that would be a no," she said with a smile. Like, a double and triple no.

Mason said nothing, shifting his attention from Camilla to her mom only briefly, her dad even less, and then back again, catching Camilla's eyes and swallowing hard. Suddenly, she was terrified at what he might say. As *normal*—and she hated to use the word—as he had seemed when he was alone with her, or after a while anyway, in front of her parents he appeared to be regressing to the way he was at the meeting in New York, apart despite being right beside them, shifting from foot to foot. Awkward.

She sympathized with Mason. The Anderson family, even a small subset, could be overwhelming and probably even more so to somebody like Mason, who wasn't used to *any* family it sounded like, let alone a family like hers, where humor and unquestionable acceptance and love were so much in the mix. And the Andersons had never been a picnic for boyfriends in any case, unless they became son-in-laws eventually. They'd never met a boss to her knowledge. And one who was a messy combination of the two... Well, that was a real worry.

Mason opened his mouth and all that came out, low and hard to hear, was, "*That* was your brother?"

Her parents stiffened and some of the sympathy she had been feeling for him dissipated.

She waited for the insensitive comment that was sure to follow. Even guys who had the requisite ability to screen themselves often pissed her off with what they might say off-handedly about her exuberant, special little brother.

And that was the kiss of death with her. One wrong word about Joey and a guy was gone as far as any of the Anderson sisters were concerned.

Her parents didn't take too kindly to it, either.

"Yes, that was Joey," her mom said, a slight tightening in her mouth.

But Mason commented no further, merely watching Joey's energetic enjoyment of an oversize chocolate chip cookie, the crumbs falling freely.

Her mother turned to Camilla. "We were thinking of having Brandy just stay back with your brother, but we didn't have the heart to lie to him, and he was as worried as we were."

"I'm glad he came, Mom. Though I'm sorry you guys had to go to so much trouble. I'm fine really."

Her dad kissed the top of her head again, and her mom captured her hand and squeezed it.

Mason turned from watching Joey back to Camilla, not making eye contact with either of her parents. "Can I have a word?"

"Sure. Of course. Excuse me for a minute, guys." She hurried after Mason, who was already striding over to the fireplace.

"Sorry about this," she said quietly when she joined him. "I know they're a little much, and you're not used to—"

He pulled her toward him, bending his head as if he was going to, ah, actually *kiss* her. In front of everybody, even though as far as her parents knew he was just her brand-new boss, and she wasn't planning on explaining anything more to them right now, or to the pilots for that matter who were beside them, done checking in, card keys in hand, all of them watching. She jerked away.

"Mason!"

He dropped his hands, not even glancing at their audience, and ran them through his hair. "I wanted to talk to you, Camilla. Be alone with you."

"Not now, for goodness sake."

"Why not?"

"Mason." She sighed, smiling over at her parents, who looked quickly away, pretending they weren't watching the exchange with her boss. "It's a family thing, okay? We'll talk later," she added, not sure how she felt about it, either. "And not a word about Joey, do you understand?"

She turned away, barely hearing his soft, "Not really."

"Mason just wanted to talk about tomorrow," she told her parents and the pilots when she went back to them, Mason a beat behind her.

"Do you need anything from us at this point, sir?" one of them asked Mason. "Or should we reconvene in the morning?"

"Morning's fine," Mason said shortly. "I don't need you. Just Camilla."

She let that last part slide.

The pilots nodded. "Pleasure to meet you, Mr. and Mrs. Anderson."

"You, too, boys," her father said. "Remember, fans for life!"

They grinned and headed to the elevator.

"I better go check in," Mason mumbled.

When he walked away, her mom's brow furrowed. "I hope it really is okay we brought Joey, Cammy. We didn't give a thought to the fact that your boss would be here. We were just so worried, but, well, we don't want to embarrass you."

"Mom, don't be ridiculous. Of course it's okay you *all* came." She kissed her cheek, still soft and unwrinkled despite her seventy years. Genetics. She glanced at Mason, who was behind one other person in line at the reception desk. At least he hadn't tried to take cuts. "I'm finding out that my new boss is kind of, ah, well, odd sometimes. But nice," she assured them. "Very nice."

Her dad frowned and kissed her hand. All this affection was even more than the amount usually poured on one of their daughters. That almost crashing in a plane thing again. She felt as cosseted as when she was five and fell out of their slow-moving station wagon, packed to the gills with Andersons. She had merited an ice cream cone and control of the TV remote for the whole night, even though it was her own fault for unbuckling her seat belt and not closing the car door properly.

"He wasn't saying something about Joey when he pulled you away, was he?" her dad demanded.

"No! Of course not! No, that was about tomorrow, like I said. Plans for tomorrow and everything."

"Hmmph. It didn't look—" He glanced at his wife, who shook her head slightly. "Never mind. Your career's your own, Cammy. You worked hard enough for it. But I will say that I know you just started, but don't you take any non-sense from a boss about *anything*, no matter how good the job. You're too smart to—"

"Daddy, don't worry." Her eyes started to tear again and she swiped them, laughing as he shook his head.

"When Carly finally told me what a sweat shop that law firm you were at was, all I could think was you should have left years ago." He glared at Mason. "And if this one's no better, I say his loss. Not everybody goes to Harvard, honey."

"A lot of them on Wall Street do, Dad. Anyway, Mason's fine." If she decided to quit, she'd revise that opinion with her dad. Not that her parents ever tried to control any of their children's career moves. If she wanted to quit a job, they'd be nothing but supportive.

Loan companies weren't so accommodating.

"I better check in myself. What about you guys?"

"We're all set. Got here about a half hour ago," her mom said. "That Miss White is so sweet. She insisted that Mr. Talbot wanted to pay for everything. And then that private jet. Ooh la la!"

Mason probably didn't even know he was paying for everything. And private jets had lost their allure for Camilla.

"Okay, hang on, I'll go check in, and then maybe we can go to an early dinner or something."

Mason was in the front of the line when she got there.

At the check-in desk, the elderly clerk hustled to get the room key, since "Mr. Talbot's assistant had taken care of all the checking-in arrangements." Apologizing that the whole party couldn't all be on the same corridor, he handed Mason the key just as her father appeared behind her, hugging her again.

"And here's your card key, Mr. Talbot, for the room for you and Miss Anderson. Our best suite on the executive VIP floor, one I like to call our Bridal Suite."

Her head whipped up to register her father's shocked expression, his face frozen.

*Room? Room?*

"Do you need a second key?" the clerk asked politely as steam came out of her ears. My God, how could Mason have put them in one room without even asking her? Forget about the pilots finding out, or Marcia knowing, but her parents? *Her parents!*

# Chapter Seven

"Room?" Camilla asked. "I think you mean the plural. Rooms. As in one for each of us."

"I'll go see what Brandy and Joey are up to," her dad mumbled, wandering off.

The clerk looked uncomfortably between her and Mason. "I'm sorry. I thought Mr. Talbot's assistant specified one room for the both of you. The best we had."

With the glare Talbot was giving the clerk now, she wouldn't be surprised if he bought the whole hotel chain to fire the poor guy. He had probably instructed Marcia to tell the front desk to pretend there was only one room left or some other crap.

Good old, straightforward Mason Talbot was learning a few new tricks to go with his otherwise clueless *"Got sex?"* approach to satisfying his biological urges. Nice to know her brief tenure as his in-house counsel had accomplished something.

"I'd like a separate room," she said to the clerk. "And if you plan on claiming there's only one room left in the whole hotel, you can give me the key to it, and Mr. Talbot here can sleep on a chair in your lovely lounge there."

The clerk's helpless panicked look at Mason almost made her feel sorry for him. But Mason said nothing.

"No, we have another room of course. We have one hundred and twenty rooms in this hotel. Just not another, er, *Bridal Suite*. That's the best room we've got. The others that are left are regular singles."

"I'll take the Bridal Suite," she decided immediately, resolving to have her parents see the room was just hers and explain the "confusion" before they went to dinner. "You can give Mr. Talbot a regular room."

He deserved it for assuming she would share a room with him now that they were back in civilization *and* for not making it clear once her parents showed up that he needed different arrangements. She wasn't too happy with Marcia, either, if this was her doing. She at least should have known better.

The clerk handed her the key and she added, "And let me hasten to inform you that I'm an attorney, and if you give the key to my room to *anyone* else without my express permission, I'll sue the pants off you. Got it?"

The clerk nodded. She had planned to either invite Mason to her room to talk or go to his, maybe even invite him to dinner with her family, but his incredible gall in arranging one room made her think better of it. It was probably safer for both of them now if she just talked to him in the morning anyway. They needed some distance from each other after the intensity of the last day.

"Good night, Mr. Talbot," she said, heading toward her parents. "I'll see you in the morning."

Mason said nothing.

Yep, everything back to nice and normal.

The clerk stammered his apologies as Mason tuned him out. He was dialing Marcia.

"How did it go?" she asked as she picked up.

"Like shit. She stormed off to her own room."

"Mason! What did you say to her?"

"Nothing."

"Nothing? As in, actually nothing? None of the things you told me?"

"No."

"Well, then of course she stormed out. I told you it was very important to talk to her and say everything you said you wanted to say and *ask her* if it was okay if you shared a room, since you're traveling on business after all. Did you say any of it?"

"We didn't have a chance to even talk, since you didn't rent me a car—like you were supposed to."

"Mason." He could hear the exaggerated patience in her voice. "That wouldn't have been a very good idea even if there had been a rental place nearby. You trying to have a conversation, especially that conversation, while you were driving was a recipe for a five-car pile-up. Unless she was driving, I guess. But even then she probably would have insisted the four of you take the car, not just you and her."

"So instead we piled in some van thing, all four of us,

and next thing I know we're at the hotel, and you're talking to her on the phone as we got out. When was I exactly supposed to talk to her?"

"Before you got *in* the van. And definitely before the room clerk gave the two of you one room. Take her aside or something. How were her parents, by the way? They seem so sweet."

"Yeah, and thanks for the heads-up on that, by the way."

"I didn't want you to panic."

"I didn't," he muttered. "But they've been all over her since we got here. Taking her aside didn't exactly work."

"Come on. They're her family. Her plane crash-landed. They're going to want to reassure themselves she's okay."

"Yeah, well, my plane crash-landed, too, and I was taking care of her just fine."

"Well, all I can say is without talking to Camilla beforehand, I can imagine she didn't appreciate finding out in real time that we'd booked one room for the two of you."

"See, that's the part I don't get. We already slept together. More than once. *A lot.*"

"Mason!" Now he could hear the exaggerated *loss* of patience in her voice. "Also, are you having this conversation in front of the desk clerk?"

"Yes. Why?"

"Then you shouldn't be saying in front of him you already slept with her."

He glanced at the clerk, who was studiously eying his computer screen. "He's not listening."

"He's pretending not to listen."

"I called to find out what to do. Just get on with it," he snapped, instigating a long silence on the other end, which with Marcia was never good.

"You shouldn't even be talking to me about this," she finally said, "but I took pity on you, since you sounded, well, not like you."

"Thanks. You're all heart. So what now?" He felt more lost than when he and Camilla had been trudging forward in the mud. All he knew was he wanted to be with her, like they had been together in the last day, and it had all gone so wrong for reasons he couldn't quite understand. Her damn family was everywhere he turned, and suddenly she was back to treating him like the boss and being mad at him, like they'd started out on the plane yesterday.

"You like the woman, Mason. I've never heard you talk about anyone the way you did about her."

That annoyed him. "I don't even know what I said to you," he muttered.

"Exactly."

Another one of those long silences.

"So were you polite to her parents?"

"I don't think I even said anything."

"That's not good."

"Oh and her father was standing right next to her when she blew up about the room. Or standing there for a minute, anyway. He walked away before she got going."

"The clerk didn't say it in front of her father, did he?"

"I guess, but that wasn't the problem."

"That was sure as hell part of the problem." She sighed. "You don't know fathers and daughters."

"God, there are so many rules with this," he complained.

"Look, at this point, I'm probably doing more harm than good. You're going to have to figure this one out for yourself, my boy. Good luck."

And then she hung up on him, which surprisingly she rarely did. From the few occasions it had happened, though, he knew calling back would be fruitless. She would never answer, even if he tried it a hundred times, which he actually had once for the hell of it. Why not? He had redial.

He slipped the phone back into his pocket.

The clerk gave him his full attention now as Mason tried to think of what to do. "Miss Anderson's suite has an adjoining door to the room next to it," he offered. "I could give you the other one. The door between them *is* locked on each side," he added, probably worrying about the suing the pants threat. "But it's the best I can do."

Mason nodded. At least it was something.

When he headed toward the elevator, the Anderson family was nowhere to be seen and neither was Camilla. There was a restaurant on the ground floor, Trendz the sign said, so maybe they were all in there. He slipped the card key into his pocket, but chickened out on going in to see, pretending he wanted to eat, too. Just as well since his stomach was churning, and he doubted he could swallow a thing.

He wished he had thought of something else to say to her parents. Or the brother maybe, who seemed interesting, but he wasn't supposed to say anything about for some reason.

*All these fucking rules…*

The sister looked just like her, but a few years older.

As to her mother and father, they didn't resemble either of their daughters or the son for that matter, except for a similarity in talking and holding their heads. And laughing. There was a lot of that along with the smiles he had come to associate with Camilla. But in contrast to the long, blond hair of her daughters, Mrs. Anderson sported short, brown, curly hair, only slightly less unruly than his own, with shots of gray threaded throughout. Mr. Anderson's hair was steel gray, what was left of it, completely bald on the top, and he was tall and thin, to his wife's shorter, plumper frame. Both of them looked much younger than he suspected they must be, with six children older than Camilla.

He headed to the elevator.

He wished he was eating dinner, or late lunch or whatever, with all the Andersons right now, then taking Camilla to bed thereafter, snuggling with her in a proper king-sized bed in the Bridal Suite.

But if he could have only one thing or the other tonight, he was shocked to realize he would have preferred sitting down with her family.

Damn. What the hell was wrong with him?

Just in case, though, he went into the gift shop, hoping they had condoms.

Joey talked non-stop in the elevator on the way up to the Executive VIP floor that needed a special key to make the elevator open. *There had been nobody in the plane but them, and he hadn't been scared at all, and he wondered if Cammy was going to go on the plane home with them.* Brandy chimed in occasionally.

Her parents each held one of her hands. The huddle they had been in when she joined them from the check-in desk made her suspect that her dad had shared with her mom the surprising news from the clerk even before Camilla babbled on about the mix-up. When they all arrived at her suite, she inserted the card key in the door and invited them in, promising Joey a peek at the mini-bar though they had to wait until after dinner to raid it.

The room opened to a large sitting room, wall-to-wall windows allowing late afternoon sunlight to filter in, coating the buildings in the distance in sepia like an old-fashioned photo. Plush, cream carpet complemented the rose silk covered couches and polished wood side tables with legs that looked like lion's claws. Brandy wandered beyond the sitting room into the bedroom. "Wow, look at this. Very nice."

The bed, covered in a lacy white coverlet over more rose silk, was huge, the requisite flat screen looming nearby.

"And this bathtub," her sister added, marveling at the gleaming whirlpool tub right in the bedroom, big enough to accommodate more than the bridal couple it was supposed to, a glass blocked shower and gold countered vanity in the nearby bathroom.

Her mother took Camilla aside. "Honey, you've been through an incredible experience. Not only the plane, ah, *landing*," she apparently didn't want to say emergency landing or crash, "but it sounds like you were walking your way out of the woods all night."

Not *all* night.

"I won't have you feeling like you have to entertain us. It's enough for us to know you're safe. To see you. We couldn't have imagined a better outcome. You take a shower, or maybe a bath in this lovely tub, and get some rest. And if you still feel like a late dinner after you've taken a nap, you let us know. But I'm betting your head will hit that pillow, and you'll be out for the night."

"No, Mom, I want to go to dinner."

Her dad came over. "You listen to your parents for once, little girl, and have some alone time before we descend on you. We can catch up tomorrow."

"If this is because of what the clerk said—"

"No!"

"No! Of course not."

Their denials were simultaneous and pretty loud.

Brandy glanced over with interest from where she and Joey were taking an inventory of the mini-bar.

"Accidents happen. Mix-ups." Her mother stared intently into her eyes, and Camilla wondered if she was talking about the clerk or something else.

"Don't think a thing about it, sweetie," her dad said. "We just want you to relax, and maybe your sister will come and check on you in a little while. See how you are."

"Did you leave your suitcase in the plane?" her mom asked.

"Oh, yes." She just remembered.

"No problem. You know how Brandy over packs for everything. She'll bring you something fresh when she checks on you."

"Come on, gang," her dad called out in the direction of Brandy and Joey. "Let's leave your sister to rest."

Joey protested, but with additional hugs and kisses for all, they were gone.

As much as she wanted to be with her family, they were right. She was exhausted and needed some alone time.

But the growl emanating from her stomach reminded her she was starving. She had half a mind to call for some room service, but when she saw it was the same number as the front desk, she thought better of it after the hissy fit she had thrown with the clerk down there just now.

It was a little over the top in the outrage department, since she had already slept with Mason and might have even done so again, God help her, if they had started out with two separate rooms, sneaking behind her parents' back as the unwritten pact between the Anderson girls and their parents required. But it was the presumption that infuriated her. It was the principle of the thing. Besides, she needed her own room to steady herself—it had been pretty intense—before she talked to him again.

There was a knock on her door, and since she hadn't called for room service, she had a sneaking suspicion she knew who it was. She ought to just leave him standing out there in the hall. But she had a sudden vision of him clutching her in his arms as the plane descended and asking her all those silly questions he didn't have the slightest interest in and never would have under normal circumstances.

She opened the door.

It wasn't Mason, and she ignored the disappointment in the pit of her stomach that was worse than the hunger pains.

"Hi," her sister said, handing over neatly folded jeans and a sweater, fresh socks nestled in the bundle as well. "I'm supposed to give you these, but I think Mom and Dad sent me back here so quick to see if you wanted to talk."

Camilla shut the door, set the clothes on a chair, and went to the mini-bar to take out a Milky Way and hand Brandy a bag of popcorn. With a bottle of water for each of them, she wandered back to the bedroom and folded her legs up beneath her in the flowery armchair. "I thought they wanted me to sleep."

Brandy bounced on the bed. "I'm also supposed to make myself scarce if you really do want to be alone."

"So is this about the one room thing for me and my boss?"

"What?" Her sister burst out with a laugh. "You're kidding!"

"Oh, guess not." Mom and Dad were more circumspect than she would have thought.

"You and your boss shared one room? Was this like, when you were at the deserted ranger's station in the middle of the woods or whatever? His assistant mentioned that you'd rested at one when she called back."

Mmmm, so Marcia knew about the ranger's station. Of course she did. She'd booked the *Bridal Suite* for her boss and his new hook-up.

"That's not so bad," Brandy continued. "There was probably only one bed, right? Did you put a curtain up between you like in that old movie?"

With one bite of the caramel and chocolate, Camilla decided to come clean. Since her oldest sister, Mary, was twenty years older than she was, their parents were of a slightly older generation than the rest of her friends' parents and even if they hadn't been, they were Irish Catholics from the cradle. More like cafeteria Catholics when it came right down to it, though, adhering to the parts of the church they liked and conveniently ignoring any too strident doctrines. Camilla was pretty sure her parents didn't object in principle to their daughters having pre-marital sex so much as they didn't want to hear about it.

No such prohibition on conversation among the sisters. If not, how else would she have learned about the birds and the bees? Brandy may have been a decade older, but now that Camilla thought of it, she had first learned about the birds and the bees from this particular sister. No need to hide anything about sex from her.

Though she wished she could hide the ridiculously stupid career move. Brandy was a homemaker now, tending to her two tweens while her husband, Brad, worked as an engineer at GM, but she had been in the work force earlier, an engineer herself. She would know what a stupid thing Camilla had done by getting involved with her new boss.

"No, it wasn't in the ranger's station. I mean, it was in the ranger's station, but even before that."

"For God's sake, Cammy, it was your first day. How did you manage to fit in one time, let alone a couple? And weren't you busy almost crashing?"

Despite her sister's laugh, Camilla didn't think it was so funny right now.

"On the plane," she admitted.

"*While* it was crashing? Wow, your boss is cute, but that wouldn't have been the first thing I went for in that situation. I suppose there must have been a certain erotic allure, going out with a bang and all, but me, I would have gone for the oxygen mask instead."

"Not while it was crashing." She took a sip of the water. "Right before actually. And right after."

"You go, girl!"

"Oh stop!" But she couldn't help but smile. Sugar always made her feel better no matter how dire the circumstances. She should have lunged for a piece of candy when the plane was taking its precarious dips. And talking to a sister made her feel better. Always had. "I really screwed up, Brandy.

And I have all those loans to pay off still."

Her sister frowned. "Your boss better not be threatening to fire you, the asshole. Isn't there some legal term for that?"

"No, of course not. He didn't even seem to know sleeping with an employee was wrong at first. I had to explain it to him."

Brandy raised an eyebrow.

"Well, I am his lawyer."

She scoffed between downing handfuls of popcorn. "I didn't get to talk to him and he seems cute, but he's pulling the wool over your eyes, kid. He probably hits on women executives on their first day or something. A perverted kind of orientation."

She shook her head, certain. "No, it's not that. He's… different."

"Did *you* hit on him then?"

"No!" She took her sweater off and tossed it on the bed, then pulled her blouse out of the waistband of her jeans. "Of course not. I, ah, went along."

Her sister frowned, the laughter gone. "This doesn't sound good, Cammy. If there's something you're not telling me, if he hurt you somehow or pressured you, then you need to do something about it."

She was the one who laughed this time. "The only pressure he put on me was asking me outright if I'd sleep with him when I'd already been noticing how cute he was and was starting to even like him."

Brandy set the popcorn on the nightstand and took her hand. "That doesn't sound like you."

"I know. I can't believe I did it. I didn't fall into bed with him, into his lap I mean, right away," she hastened to add.

"First I was really mad and he tried to drop it, but I needed to explain to him that it was illegal and confirm that there were no pending, or incipient, suits."

"God, now you sound just like a lawyer." Nobody was a fan of lawyers, even in her own family.

"I am a lawyer."

"That's your problem." Brandy pushed a strand of Camilla's hair away from her eyes. "Your hair looks like shit, by the way."

She laughed and pulled her hand away, standing up. "I'm calling Carly."

"No, you don't!" She snatched the hotel cordless phone up. "I was the closest one locally when Mom and Dad were a nervous wreck. You know how Dad always said his worst nightmare would be to lose a child, and he prays to God he dies before any of us do. So I'm the one who was on the plane reassuring them to keep their hopes up and keeping Joey from getting scared."

"I know, I know." Camilla leaned down to hug her. "And I'm so thankful."

"Hmmph," her sister huffed. "Dee Dee wanted to come, but she was getting her hair highlighted today."

Camilla slapped at her arm, both of them laughing. "You are so mean!"

"I'm kidding of course. Dee Dee, everybody, was terrified. But no calling Carly. Why should she get all the juicy stuff? I'm older than her anyway." She relinquished the phone, tossing it aside. "But I have to tell you, honey, that lecturing the man about not having sex with you after his proposition, while you were alone, was probably not the wisest idea."

"Why not?" she objected, kicking off the clunky boots she realized she still had on. "I had to. It was my fiduciary obligation to my client."

"Because for one thing, talking about sex, no matter what the context, tends to keep a man's mind on it. You could have maybe cooled down a little and written him a memo about it."

"I didn't think of it that way. I was just so mad. And then," she glanced at her sister, turning her back to get this part out, "then I had a few scotches."

Brandy was back to laughing. "You are such an easy drunk."

"I am not! I never even drink at work functions, and I can't think of the last time I've been in a bar."

"Now you know why."

"I need to clean up." Camilla went to the bathroom and stripped off the rest of her clothes before putting on the robe provided with the suite.

Her sister wandered in as she washed her face with the hotel soap.

"Be sure to put some conditioner on there when you get in the shower. Your hair looks like a bird's nest."

She scrubbed at the remaining amount of grime the woods had left on her face. "You know I almost would have preferred Mom in here talking about this to me."

Brandy leaned back against the sink. "Huh! I still re-member when she actually tried to talk to us about this kind of thing. It was painful. You're so lucky by the time they got to you they passed the buck and delegated this kind of thing to us older girls."

Patting a towel against her face, Camilla turned on the

shower. "Apparently, it's an emergency I wash my hair, so scoot. Either come back later, or go amuse yourself in the sitting room."

"Come back later? Are you kidding? I got to hear the rest of this. I wouldn't leave now if my life depended on it. Or one of my kids called."

Camilla closed the bathroom door on her. With the steaming hot shower, the muscle relaxing water pressure, and the comforting presence of her sister right outside, very welcome despite the wise cracks, since she needed to talk this out, she felt better altogether. A few minutes later, she came out and went into the sitting room, her wet hair in a towel, the fluffy cotton robe snug and warm around her. Her sister was talking in low tones at the door.

"Brandy? What is it?"

"Just Dad." She stepped away to show her father hovering in the doorway, giving his older daughter a brief annoyed look. "He's checking up on us, Cammy. Or more to the point, on you."

"I wanted to make sure everything was okay, honey. Your sister answered my text saying you were in the shower, and so I thought I'd pop up and just double-check with her you didn't need anything."

And undoubtedly make sure she wasn't having a nervous breakdown. "Daddy, I am absolutely fine."

"I know, I know. Let your father worry about you a little, under the circumstances."

"Of course," she said softly. "Why don't I get dressed, and we'll all go to dinner after all?"

He rolled his eyes. "Are you kidding? Your mother would be mad I came up here at all. I told her I was going down to the gift shop for some cigarettes."

"You don't smoke."

"I think she was so grateful to get me out of the room, she didn't question it."

Camilla went into his arms, and he patted her shoulder. "Ignore your anxious father."

"You know us, Dad," Brandy said. "We're just down-loading. I'll be back to the room in a little bit, and we can go to dinner and leave Cammy to sleep. I think she does need it. It sounds like the last day has been pretty, ah, *strenuous.*"

Camilla didn't even crack a smile.

"Sounds good. Breakfast tomorrow morning?" her father asked her.

"Absolutely," Camilla answered.

When he was gone, she noticed through the windows that the afternoon sun had mellowed into impending darkness, though it was still early. She turned on a few lamps, resulting in a soft muted lighting presumably meant to foster romance, and then she sat on the couch next to her sister.

"So," Brandy said. "Before I go do double-duty and calm our parents down again on your behalf—"

"I'll go to dinner!"

"No, Cammy. You don't need an Anderson production tonight. You can appear all refreshed tomorrow morning at breakfast and reassure Mom and Dad that you're a big girl and everything is fine. Tonight you have to take for yourself. To think, or whatever," she said ambiguously.

Camilla shrugged. "Not much to think about in one sense. I can't stay at a job where I've had sex with my boss, especially since he's the CEO. It taints everything, my position, my legitimacy as an adviser."

"I'm not talking about your job, Cammy," she said with a dismissive shake of her hair, which looked fabulous by the way.

"Well, I am. That's what I'm talking about."

"What you should be talking about is what you think of this Talbot guy, since you had sex with him, more than once, which is something to my knowledge you don't do very often—or at all lately." She hastened to add, "And if you and Carly have been holding back on me, you're in trouble."

Camilla brought her knees up. "No, you're right. I haven't. Maybe that's why I went combustible all the sudden. Like dry tinder with a spark of something. Mason was just the…lighter."

Her sister tilted her head. "Is that how it was? You didn't, ah, simply like the guy."

She was silent, trying to figure out how to answer that. She ended up deciding on honesty. "I liked him a lot."

Brandy nodded. "So that's what you should be thinking about now. The two of you."

"There is no two of us. You don't understand, he's… He's never even had a girlfriend."

"My God! You popped your boss's cherry?"

"No," she muttered. "Of course not."

"Good, because that wouldn't have been normal for a guy that age. I'd be guessing gay."

"Not that it's any of your business, but he was very hot in bed."

"Of course it's not my business. Tell me more."

Camilla flipped her head and toweled her hair. "He doesn't have relationships."

"That's what they all say. Believe me. Brad was saying

that right up to the altar."

"No, he's odd…different."

Brandy eyed her. "*Different…* So what's wrong with that?"

"He didn't even know what to say to Mom and Dad."

"What boyfriend does the first time?"

"He's not my boyfriend." She rubbed her hair more vigorously. "You don't understand."

"Do you like him or not, Cammy?" Brandy persisted.

"Yes, I like him, but I don't think it's in the cards. It's not just that he's different, it's that we're too different, from each other."

Brandy took the comb she had brought out of the bathroom with her and tugged it gently through Camilla's wet hair, a soothing motion that reminded her of childhood, one sister or another getting her ready for school, her mother the general overseeing the process, making lunches, calling out instructions.

Had it really been so easy then? Probably not. A few years after she was born Joey came, and life wasn't easy after that. Wonderful, but not easy.

Which reminded her of the question Mason had asked. The only question. If that was her brother.

"He's so awkward with people sometimes. I wonder how he would really take Joey."

The comb paused. "Well, fuck him then."

And they both laughed. Once her hair was smooth, Brandy handed her back the comb and stood up. "Don't you think you should give him a chance and you'll see? He might surprise you."

She leaned over and kissed Camilla's cheek. "Sounds

like you need to talk, you two."

"What do I do about my job?"

Brandy folded her arms across a chest that was heading slightly in their mother's direction, perfectly comfortable with the ten extra pounds she had put on since her marriage. Like most of her sisters, Brandy was happy. What was wrong with Camilla that she was not, even with all the love surrounding her?

"Get a new job. Or better yet, do something else. I hate to say this, Cammy, but you've never liked being a lawyer."

"Feel free to say it," she muttered. "I say it all the time."

"Exactly. Even when we flew out to Reno—"

"Oh, don't bring that up again." She flopped against the back of the couch. "I know, I know, I get flirty when I drink."

"That wasn't what I was going to say." Her blue green eyes were serious. "I was going to say that there you were, just passed the bar, had a lucrative high-paying job on Wall Street and, honey, you *were not* happy. In fact, though you tried to hide it, you were desperately *unhappy*, and I've always thought that was because you felt like you were closing a door, not opening one."

"You don't understand about all the student loans I had to take out."

Brandy headed to the door. "No, I guess I don't. Because I care more about whether my little sister is happy than I do about whether she defaults on her student loans."

"They're not dischargeable in bankruptcy," she called to her departing form as Brandy gave one last wave and left.

A minute or two later, there was another knock. "What did you forget to lecture me about?"

She opened the door.

"Hi," Mason said.

"Hi." She leaned against the doorjamb. "I suppose the desk clerk gave you my room number."

"He gave me the room next door, too." He nodded to it. "The one adjoining this one."

"Lawsuit thing scared him, I see."

"It did. The door's locked."

"So you really did have to knock."

"Yes, but I chose to knock on the front door, not the adjoining one."

"That was very wise of you. You aren't as slow on the uptake as you seem."

He smiled and a rush of unwise, extremely unwise, affection for him overtook her senses. "You're teasing me again," he said softly.

"That or insulting you. I haven't decided which."

"Will you come out and talk to me?"

Again, another surprisingly wise move on his part, instead of asking to come in or asking her to come to his room. The cluelessness probably was all an act, despite what she had earnestly assured Brandy. He had been very good at the actual sex part.

*Remembering that fact was so not helping.*

# Chapter Eight

"No, come on in. We do have to talk, and we should do it privately."

He was pretty tentative about it and didn't sit on the couch, as Brandy had, choosing a nearby chair instead. Probably Marcia had coached him on everything.

At the thought, she said, "I know I seem like I've been a bitch since we got to the hotel, but the truth is, with my family around and everything, I'm realizing I didn't feel like myself through that whole time with you. And I'm not sure I liked it."

"Neither did I. But I liked it very much."

She steeled herself. "I *am* going to quit. This doesn't change that. In fact, do I really have to get on a plane and go to the UK? I'd rather not."

He shook his head. "No, that's fine."

Immediately annoyed he was taking her definitive move to quit so easily, she taunted, "What? Did Marcia tell you I had to resign now, since I slept with you and everything?"

"We didn't talk about that."

"I bet. Getting good at lots of normal guy moves, aren't you? If you ever weren't, that is. Lying now. Great." *She defended him with her sister, but attacked him when they were alone?* She was a bundle of contradictions with this guy.

Sort of like him. So sweet and sexy when they were alone or making love and so aloof and awkward a lot of the rest of the time.

"Marcia and I didn't talk about you quitting. We talked about everything else."

"You told her I cried when we were crashing!" Okay, she was really pissed now. A matter of personal pride nobody but possibly another Anderson sister might understand.

"What? No, of course not. Why would she care about that anyway? I almost cried myself."

"You did not. You were Mr. CEO himself, all calm and cool. I was jealous at how you kept your head. Made me look like a total wimp in comparison." She added quickly, because she wasn't much of a liar herself, "But it was very comforting. Don't get me wrong."

"Marcia told me to tell you what I'd told her, but apparently, I got the timing wrong. It was supposed to be before you knew I wanted to share the Bridal Suite." He looked around at the lavish sitting room, the picture window. "Which I can assure you is much nicer than the room next door."

"What happened on the plane in the first place was a mistake."

"Yes, clearly the weather information they premised the flight on was faulty. That storm was supposed to dissipate by the time it caught up to us. I assume we shouldn't have taken off at all."

"The sex! The sex with you was a mistake."

He said nothing.

"What, didn't Marcia feed you some lines here?"

She'd be pounding the pavement trying to explain this fiasco of a job on her resume, and he'd move on to some other blonde who was more accommodating to his biological urges.

"Christ, there are all these rules, and I don't understand half of what you *or* Marcia is telling me. I just know—"

She waited for a long time for the end of that sentence as he got up and went over to the window with its view of early evening darkness, no moon even.

She should show him out now. She'd said everything she meant to say. She was quitting. She didn't want to go to the UK. She wasn't a baby who cried at the drop of a hat…or the drop of a plane for that matter. Normally.

Putting a palm to her stomach at the sick feeling engendered by the memory of the plane almost crashing, she wondered if he was thinking about that, too. About how they were lucky to be alive.

Always, even if they only realized it in brief chunks of moments.

And why was she going to show him out of the room again?

"All I know is that I want to be with you, Camilla. And I'm not talking about sex," he added, turning back to her. "Fuck the sex. Forget about sex. That's not what I'm talking about. I don't care what anybody wanted to be when they grow up."

His confessions were kind of getting to her. "There were unusual circumstances involved when you asked me that Mason."

"What unusual circumstances?"

"We thought the plane was crashing. You were trying to help me get my mind off it. You didn't really care."

"That's right. I never care, but I did then. And I do. I do right now. I feel bad you wanted to be a pilot."

"Believe me, I'm over it. Especially after yesterday."

"Or that you don't like being a lawyer."

"Everybody hates their job," she said with the automatic consolation she used to justify the stupidity of taking out hundreds of thousands of dollars of loans to become something it turned out she hated. "I'm just on the far end of that spectrum."

"No, everybody doesn't hate their job. Well, actually, I don't know that. I know I don't hate my job."

The billionaire exception again.

"And I don't know if anybody else does, because sincerely I have never given a fuck. Really."

She laughed. "I believe you."

"But I do with you. That's what I'm trying to say. I do. I don't know why."

"Maybe because we went through a plane crash together," she offered, "or almost, I mean. It's a post-traumatic stress thing."

"No, I cared before. You said you hated your job before that, and I wondered why you didn't do something else."

"The crushing debt load," she said.

"I know. I know. But the point is I even wondered. And I'd like to talk to your brother Joey. See? My God, I even remembered *his* name." He was laughing and shaking his head.

She didn't quite know what to say. She tried to remember this was the guy who casually commented that he wouldn't mind marrying her so he could have a steady stream of sex with someone to whom he was attracted. He wasn't really the sexy, sweet guy he'd been before they screeched to a halt on the runway or as they trekked along side by side on the muddy trail. He was a nutty, introverted *billionaire* who wouldn't be giving her the time of day if his biological urges hadn't been primed just right.

Time to bring that guy back to the conversation.

"Joey's the youngest, and my mom was older when she had him. He had a loss of oxygen when he was in the womb," she said, making it sound as callous as she could. "I don't know his actual IQ, but let's just say I don't see you having a lot in common with him."

"I don't have a lot in common with anybody," Mason said right away, not pausing a beat. "And I'm sorry about the oxygen thing, but normal's not all it's cracked up to be anyway. And, see the thing is, if you think he's great, I think he must be then. You see, that's it! That's the thing!"

If Mason Talbot wasn't understanding her or Marcia, she had to admit she wasn't quite understanding him here, either. He was saying, "that's the thing" and "that's it" and giving it the enthusiasm of a "Eureka!"

"I can't believe anyone would be perpetually disappointed in you, Camilla. That's what I'm saying."

She had forgotten she had even said that to him about her parents. It wasn't true. They were never disappointed in her, in any of them, even Joey. Especially not Joey. "I was being a bitch there. My parents aren't disappointed in me. If anything, I'm disappointed in myself for the choices I've made. I valued trying to look like I was smart and making money over what I really wanted to do."

She shouldn't have disclosed that last part.

"What did you want to do?" he asked. "It wasn't become a pilot?"

She wished she had managed to limit the confessions here to him. But what the hell? She should give him something.

"I wanted to be a writer," she admitted. "Pathetic, huh? Me and twenty million other English majors."

"I doubt twenty million people major in English."

"It's a turn of phrase." She shook her head and held a hand up to the throbbing temple to ease the pounding headache she felt coming on.

"And it's nowhere near pathetic."

"What are you trying to say?"

And then he ruined it all.

"I'm trying to say I want to have sex with you again…"

Yep, there he was. She really had to get to showing him the door. "Thanks for bringing me back to reality."

But he added, "And I am trying to say that. I am. But it's the fact that I want to. I don't know why and maybe it's biology or chemistry or whatever, but I don't feel like myself at all when I'm with you, and I hate it and I like it and I want it. I want you. Not to be my lawyer, and that's not because you slept with me. It's because you hate it, and I don't want you to hate it. I just want you to be with me. Whatever it takes."

"Hmmm. Is Marcia going to be calling my cell now, offering me a million dollars if I stay with you?" she joked. "At least that would take care of my student loans, and it'd be just chump change for you."

"Is that an option?"

"No!" She threw up her arms in exasperation.

"I was just asking." He smiled when he said it.

"What does Marcia say about all this?" she asked, feeling defensive that he had discussed her with his uber-assistant.

He scoffed, looking out the window again. "I don't believe everything Marcia tells me."

"What? What does she tell you? I'm a gold digger?"

He looked back at her, his big, blue eyes so beautiful. "She says I'm in love with you."

He hurried on. "But of course that's ridiculous because I don't believe in love. And especially not love at first sight. Not that it would have been first sight with you because I barely noticed you then. Not in the office, not really, although you were doing that thing with the pearls that was incredibly hot."

She'd have to work with him on that ruining thing.

"That's okay. I don't believe in it, either," she lied. She did. Of course she did. What child of two people happily married for fifty years didn't believe in love?

One of them wasn't like, well, like Mason was. Or even, like, well, like she was.

And she and Mason weren't in love.

He took her chin in his strong, warm hand and kissed her, long and tenderly, his other hand sifting through her wet hair, undoing Brandy's efforts. It was tingly and nice and special.

And for the first time, some hope for them welled up in her chest.

"But I feel something for you," he whispered against her ear. "I do."

"Don't ask me if we can have sex again," she begged. "You'll ruin it."

He dropped his hands from her face and said, "I won't. I'll go back to my room now, and you can go out to dinner with your family or whatever you were going to do, and we'll talk about all this tomorrow. Okay? We'll talk."

He was so sincere she laughed. "Don't go. My family told me I should sleep. They're not expecting me for dinner."

"They aren't?"

"No, but I'm starving. Why don't you order some room service? A burger and fries for me and then whatever you want."

She listened as he picked up the phone and fumbled through it, proud of him for not calling Marcia to coach him.

When he hung up, he said, "About a half hour. Maybe more. Apparently, they're busy."

"Perfect. So while we're waiting... We *can* have sex again. In fact, I'm insisting on it. Just don't ask again, okay?"

What she didn't tell him was that it might be the last time. For a while anyway. She had to make up her mind what to do about this situation. Just as she was a modern feminist who didn't sleep with the boss her first day on the job—uh, well, she didn't *believe* in doing it anyway—she also didn't believe in letting Price Charming —or in this case, Prince *UnCharming*—sweep her and her student loans off her feet.

She had to figure this out for herself.

But she wanted him. Now. Again.

He narrowed his eyes at her as she tugged him into the bedroom. "This isn't some kind of trick question or test, is it?

Because I really have had a tough two days. You can cut me a break, can't you?"

"Absolutely."

She texted Brandy to say she was going to "sleep"—putting it in quotes to give Brandy a sense that something else might be going on—and to call the room if she needed to get a hold of her. Then she switched off her phone and threw her arms around his neck, loving the way he leaned into her, his whole body becoming loose and fluid, the tension draining from him.

"Well, I've had a wonderful two days. Except for the plane crash, I mean. A really fabulous, cool, special two days."

She kissed him and he murmured, "Me, too. Me, too."

He pushed her to the bed and climbed on top of her, loosening the tie to her robe and slipping his hand inside, warm against her hip. "You smell all nice and clean."

"I took a shower. It felt great."

"I haven't taken mine yet." His hand slid lower. "I really should, but since you still have no underwear on, I'm having trouble summoning up the will to."

"What if I take one with you?"

He grinned. "Perfect. Let me go back to my room for a second first."

She pushed him off gently. "Uh-uh. You won't need anything for this shower. Don't go getting any ideas."

She slipped the robe off her shoulders, letting it fall to the floor as she led him to the bathroom.

"I'm getting ideas already, believe me."

She turned on the nozzle in the shower until steam came out, and when she glanced back at him, he was naked and ready. For more than a shower, his cock hard and throbbing, his eyes intense. They stepped under the water together, the shower roomy enough for both of them, a stool for sitting built into one corner.

She took command of the soap and washed his lean, muscular body with long leisurely strokes that left him breathing hard, one side of his mouth coming up. "Do I get a chance with that?" he asked.

"Nope. Turn around."

As she lingered on his taut buns, he placed his palms on the tiles, dropping his head, and she went on tippy-toes to whisper in his ear, "I'm reminded I owe somebody a blow job."

He groaned.

She urged him to the stool and placed a towel from the rack on the floor, kneeling down. He widened his legs so she came between them, her hands on his thighs. The hot stream of the shower beat on her back, and his eager cock reared inches from her mouth as he ran his thumbs along her lips, her cheeks.

She smiled, drawing the moment out. "*Blow job*. I take it from that look of anticipation on your, er," she leaned closer to his erection, "*face*, that you've heard that term as well?"

"Any term for fellatio is firmly imprinted on my mind. Said once, I never forget it."

"Mmmm, very much like a regular guy in that respect."

She gripped the base of his cock, her hands still slippery from the soap, and took one long swipe, flicking her tongue over the head. He gasped as she rubbed and licked, leaning closer to take him farther into her mouth with each light pass around.

When he was hunched over with the pleasure of it, she

took him as far down her throat as she could, keeping her eyes on him, reveling in the expression of ecstasy on his face. He dug his fingers into her wet hair, his whole body straining, as he watched her. Giving himself over to her, he murmured how good it felt, how sexy she was, how hot she made him.

She cupped his balls as she worked him, and he arched with a low groan.

"I'm close," he muttered. "Very close. Should I—"

She sucked harder, feeling his surrender in a hot pulse against her tongue, her throat as he came with a hoarse cry, clutching her head to him, ever closer. She swallowed and he collapsed back on the stool.

"I think I was supposed to ask first about that last part," he panted.

"Rules are made to be broken, remember?"

Smiling, very pleased to see him lose control for once, she stood, kicking the wet towel on the floor to the side, and after a minute he got to his feet as well, putting his arms around her from behind and whispering in her ear, "I've never *gotten off* like that with another woman."

She laughed. "Mmmm, am I going to hear all the sex slang you know now?"

"Only if you'll talk dirty back to me. I love to pick up new vocabulary."

He took the soap and washed her thoroughly, though she assured him she'd already bathed, lingering over her nipples, her breasts, between her legs, kissing her lightly, her body tingling from the caresses.

When they got out of the shower and dried each other off, long teasing motions, and wandered back into the bedroom, she said, "You don't by any chance have more condoms, do you?"

He smiled. "As a matter of fact, I do."

"You must have had quite a few in that wallet of yours."

"I stopped in the gift shop before I came up. Even though you were cold-shouldering me then, hope springs eternal and all that. They're next door."

She opened the adjoining door between their rooms. "Let's say we leave this open all night, shall we?"

Later, much later, after they had voraciously eaten the room service and made love again, she lay in his arms, completely full in all sense of the word, and he asked, "So what's the next step? Should we go back to New York? I can call the meeting in London off, and we can decide — "

"Shhh." She kissed him silent. "Let's not talk about tomorrow."


Rays of orange sunlight peeked through the window, and the clock read eight a.m. After switching on her phone, she saw five voicemails, one from each of her sisters who weren't here. How sweet. She'd listen to them later.

Since there was also a text from Brandy fifteen minutes before that they were going down to breakfast, she left Mason sleeping in her bed and dressed to join them.

Her father rose when she entered the restaurant and kissed her on the cheek. "I thought we were going to have to send Joey up there to wake you up. Good sleep, honey?"

"Great. Thanks, Dad. I'm starved."

"You look so much better." Her mom patted her hand as she slid between them, Brandy and Joey on the other side.

"I feel better."

Brandy watched her with a closed lip smile, and Camilla blushed at the scrutiny.

"Well, I, for one, have to get back to Detroit, guys," her sister said. "As much fun as this little interlude has been, Mikey had a spelling test and got a *D* on it, and hubby is blaming it on my absence, now that he knows you're okay."

"What do they need to be expert spellers for these days?" her dad asked, sprinkling pepper on his fried eggs as the waitress noticed Camilla and came over to take her order. She asked for an omelet, extra cheesy, and rye toast with coffee. Joey was digging into a cinnamon roll, and French toast with more syrup than bread was waiting for his attention.

"Isn't there spell check now?" her dad continued.

"You know what, Cammy?" Joey said between mouthfuls. "I got licorice from the store over there this morning."

"But you're saving it for the plane ride home," their mom reminded him before turning to Brandy. "I hope Brad isn't going to make Mikey feel bad about his grade. That just compounds itself, you know. You have to give positive reinforcement."

"I know, Mom."

They were all talking at once, a mere echo of the true cacophony that could abound when the entire family was present, principals and spouses and children, generations of similar voices all talking to and with and over each other.

Camilla soaked it in, smiling. Though she spoke with her family on the phone often, it had been too long since she had been home. Three months at least.

Mason entered the restaurant, his clothes the same as the ones he had worn the day before, his hair a mass of curls.

He searched her out as if she were a beacon in a stormy sea and nodded when he saw her, heading for their table. He looked hesitant and adorable, and her heart beat faster at the sight of him. Nervous as she was to have him interact with her family, she was glad that he was making the effort to come down and join them. Her father rose from his chair when he got there. "Mr. Talbot."

He regarded the outstretched hand, and after a slight hesitation, took it. "Good morning, sir."

She smiled at him. "Pull up a chair."

A waitress brought him an extra chair, and he ordered coffee.

"Hey." Joey leaned over Brandy to get at him. "Are you Cammy's boss?"

"Yes." Though Mason was pale and tapping his fingers against the napkin holder, he was obviously trying, looking over at her brother. "And you must be Joey."

He grinned wide. "I am. I'm Cammy's brother and Brandy's brother and Carly's brother and—"

"You don't need to go through everybody, Joey," Camilla said quickly with a laugh.

"I know all their telephone numbers, too," he said. "Maybe I can have yours? What did you say your name was again?"

"Mason." Louder this time.

Brandy snuck a pinch of Joey's sweet roll, knowing that would get his attention, and he laughed, slapping her hand away. "Hey, that's mine! You get your own."

He went back to chomping on his breakfast before his sister could try to get to it again.

Mason tapped a fork against the table edge, then his

coffee cup. An intense study of the salt shaker was next.

"So," her father tried to keep the conversation going, "you're CEO of your own company?"

"Yes."

"How's that?" her mother asked as everybody but Joey stared at Mason.

"Fine. Just fine."

"Dad and Mom were teachers," Brandy offered.

"Mmmm."

The waitress poured his coffee and he drank it, both hands clutched around the cup, blowing on the steaming brew, taking his time and devoting all his concentration to it as if it were the most difficult production problem he'd ever encountered.

Brandy caught Camilla's eyes, and they smiled at each other, a joint recognition of how nervous Mason was.

"What did your parents do, Mason?" her father asked. "Is it a family business?"

"No, it's a billion dollar public company—I don't have the exact figure for the shareholder value at this minute—and my mother was an actress."

Whoa. That was a surprise. The actress part.

"My father was a sperm donor."

Both her mom and dad dropped their mouths open, and her dad squirmed a little, saying, "Hmmph."

"What's a sperm?" Joey piped up with, picking the worst moment to join the conversation.

"It's the male reproductive cell deriving from the Greek word—"

"Thank you," her mom said loudly as her dad narrowed his eyes and blew out his cheeks. "I don't think we need to go into that right now."

Mason darted his eyes back to Camilla, as if for direction. Any minute now he'd be calling Marcia.

"Did I tell you, Joey, that when Mason and I were in the park, we saw a bear?"

"A bear?" Joey laughed. "Like a teddy bear?"

"You saw a bear, Cammy?" her mother said, not laughing.

"We did and Mason was going to beat it off with a big stick."

"That probably would not have not worked," Mason pointed out. "But it looked relatively small—"

"As far as bears go," she added.

"—although large enough to maim us."

"Enough of the bear," her mother snapped at her. "I was worried sick as it was."

"What's a sperm?" Joey asked again, and her father shifted in his seat.

"More coffee please?" he called to the waitress who was passing by.

Brandy spoke in low tones to Joey, while Mason asked Camilla, "Am I not supposed to answer that?"

Both her parents regarded Mason as if he were making a smart-alecky joke, flashing him identical looks of thinned lips and narrowed eyes, suspicious he was making fun of Joey or Joey's question at any rate.

Camilla said quickly, "Mason doesn't have any siblings."

"Hmmm," her father said. "I think even only children know that there are certain things you don't discuss at the breakfast table, in front of *ladies*."

That last part was issued in a challenging way, staring at Mason as if daring him to suggest Jack Anderson's wife and daughters were not ladies.

"How was it being an only child?" Brandy asked, trying to come to Mason's rescue. "I often thought as a kid, sharing hand-me-downs—"

"With seven girls, what in heaven's name were we supposed to do with the clothes once one grew out of something and the other was the perfect size for it?" their mother interrupted, smiling at Mason. She was often a swing vote on the boyfriend interrogation and used her power freely, going from one side to the other. Not that her parents thought he was her boyfriend of course.

"I guess it would depend on the condition of the clothing," Mason answered, freezing the older woman's smile. "I imagine the concept of diminishing returns starts to figure in at some point."

"Mason actually spent a lot of time at boarding school," Camilla jumped in, only remembering at the last minute this was a sore subject for her parents, who had been advised time and again to send Joey away to a group home and who were just as adamant about keeping him with them.

"I never understood how a parent could send their child away," her father said quietly.

"Statistics actually support—" Mason began, and Jack Anderson didn't wait for the end of the thought.

"I'm not talking about statistics," he said, gesturing with his fork to Joey. "I'm talking about real life. Real people." He added in an undertone, cutting into his hash browns, "Which some people don't know much about, I suspect."

The table was, for an Anderson meal, uncharacteristically silent.

"We should probably get going," her dad said, laying his

fork down. "Brandy has to get back."

"You're not finished with your eggs," her mother admitted.

"We can get something on the way." He gestured to the waitress for the bill, glanced at it, then handed over several tens with a smile and a short nod.

"We're taking a plane, Dad, not driving. But I guess you're right. That jet had such yummy snacks anyway." Brandy smiled again at Mason as she started to pull Joey up with her. "Let's go. Daddy wants to get going."

"Well, very nice to meet you, Mr. Talbot." Her mother started to rise as well.

"Yes," her father said without enthusiasm.

"I don't want to go!" Joey objected to getting up from the table before he had a clean plate, but Brandy tugged at his hand.

"Come on, kiddo. Don't you want to say hi to Mikey when Mom and Dad drop me off? If you do, we have to get home before he's off to soccer practice."

"What room are you in, Mom?" Camilla asked. "I'll be right up to say good-bye."

"No! I don't want to go yet," Joey said loudly. With his resistance and huffing, as well as expressive hand gestures meant to convey how upset he was at the early departure, he managed to jar against Brandy's plate of half-eaten scrambled eggs and jellied toast enough to tip it into Mason's lap.

Mason popped up, startled. "Shit!"

And the plate went crashing to the floor in a spectacular burst of noise, with the shattered pieces at his feet as he stared down, his lap a smear of yellow goop and strawberry jam.

# Chapter Nine

Joey's eyes widened and welled up with tears. "I didn't mean to! I'm sorry! I didn't mean to! And he swore!"

When Joey got to crying, well maybe the Anderson daughters didn't resort to tears anymore, but their brother was pretty good at it. The whole restaurant craned their necks in the direction of the uninhibited wails, and Brandy and her mother simultaneously flanked Joey, patting his back and telling him to calm down, assuring him it had been an accident.

"You okay there?" her father asked Mason gruffly.

Joey surged forward, a master at getting in someone's face when he wanted to, his black-framed glasses no more than a few inches from Mason's surprised blue eyes. "Listen, Mr. Mason, I didn't mean—"

At the sudden confrontation, Mason stumbled back a little, flinching, and all the Andersons, including Camilla, stared at him, mouths tight.

There was an awkward silence as her mom urged Joey back. "I'm sorry. My son is very demonstrative. He gets upset. But he doesn't mean anything by it."

All it would take to smooth the moment over would be a few words from Mason. *No problem. I understand.* Anything. Even a smile.

But all he did was shake his head, reaching for a napkin, his face shuttered.

Camilla put a hand on her brother's shoulder. "Don't worry, Joey. It's no big deal. It's not like a plane crashing."

Joey fixed his watery eyes on her, a corner of his mouth going up. "That's right. I crashed a plate, not a plane."

Brandy took his arm and led Joey away, murmuring to him, and their father said, "Sorry about that. We better get going. Thanks again. Cammy, see you upstairs." And then he was gone.

"I'll take care of this mess, Mom," Camilla assured her. "You go pack up. What room are you in?"

When she'd given the number, her mother said softly, "Thank you again, Mr. Talbot, for flying us in. It meant a lot to us. You didn't have to do that."

Camilla bit her tongue from saying that he didn't, his secretary did.

"We'll get out of your hair now."

He nodded.

When she was gone, Camilla scooped up large chunks of the broken mess, but the waitress came over and waved her off. "Don't bother. We'll sweep it all up. That was your brother?"

"Yes."

"A nice smile that boy has."

Mason was still staring down at his pants, as if not sure what to do at this point. He mumbled, "I'll call Marcia."

"You still want your omelet, miss? If so, I can move you to another table."

"No, that's all right. I'm not hungry anymore."

After the waitress left, Camilla nodded at him with a short, "I have to go. I'll see you in a bit," and strode to the exit.

He caught up to her, but she shrugged him away, avoiding his eyes. "I have to see my parents off, Mason. You better call about getting some fresh clothes."

When she went upstairs, her dad opened to her knock, shaking his head as he showed her in. "I don't know about that guy, Cammy."

She bit her lip.

"Looked like he was afraid of catching something from Joey, for God's sake," he scowled.

"We're pretty overwhelming as a group, Jack," his wife reminded him, zipping a small carry-on bag and getting up from the bed. "We forget that sometimes. And he's just her boss. It's not like we'll probably ever see him again. Right, Cammy?"

"Yes." Her voice came out thin. "That's right."

"He was simply trying to have breakfast," her mother continued, handing the carry-on to her husband and making a last minute survey of the room to make sure they hadn't left anything, opening the closet, checking under the bed. "He probably didn't expect his lawyer's whole family to show up and cause a ruckus."

"Then he shouldn't have been flying our daughter around in the middle of a goddamn storm. And *he* sat down to breakfast with us." He slung the carry-on over his shoulder. "Talking about sperm donors, for heaven sake, and taking a little accident like it was the end of the world. And what was that stuff about one room when you were checking in?" he asked Camilla, as if he been holding the question in and Mason's behavior at breakfast pried it loose. "If he was trying to pull some stunt on you when you'd just been through such a harrowing experience, I swear—"

"Daddy, I told you that was nothing," she assured him, a hand to his arm. "A mistake. Now I'm sorry about breakfast. He's not used to family, and he isn't the most outgoing guy to begin with."

"Seems like a kook," her father muttered as her mother came out of the bathroom with a plastic bag of toiletries and put them in the outside pocket of the carry-on bag. "I have half a mind to buy our own tickets home. Not go in his fancy jet."

"Daddy, please. Don't go to that trouble. I don't want to be responsible for that expense." On their retirement stipend, they couldn't afford such an out-of-the-blue cost.

"We wanted to see you, honey," he insisted. "God, when I think—"

"Yes, we did, Jack, and Mr. Talbot's office was extremely considerate to have flown us here," her mother insisted, linking arms with him. "I'm not going to make some fool gesture by not accepting their graciousness on the way home."

"You call that gracious?" he asked, with a roll of his eyes.

"Not everyone is comfortable with people who are different, Jack," her mother said quietly. "You know that."

"Maybe, but I don't have to like it."

"I don't know if that's what it was," Camilla said in a

small voice.

They waited, expecting her to say something else, arms linked, and when she didn't, whatever her face said, her mother went back over to her. "Now listen to me, honey, do you think you could take a few days to recover? I know it was your first day, but—"

"Some first day! She ought to sue the guy."

"Dad."

Her father relented. "Your mother's right. Why don't you come back with us? Clear your mind. Just for a few days."

"I do want to come home. Maybe for longer than a few days if I can swing it. If that's okay with you."

Her parents traded looks. "Of course," they said at the same time.

She had just realized that was what she wanted to do, for now, while she tried to straighten out a life that had become suddenly too messy. "But I can't come with you right now. I have to tie things up here. I'll let you know, okay?"

They went into the hall where Brandy waited with Joey, small overnight bags in their hands. Camilla gave her brother a big hug. Then her sister.

"You okay?" Brandy asked.

"I guess." Her parents stood over to the side with Joey, and she whispered, "I don't know, Brandy. Dad and Mom hate him."

"Dad is just suspicious because of the room thing, and you know how protective they are of Joey. I'm sure your, er, boss or guy or whatever didn't mean anything. I don't know. I've given you my best advice. I guess you can poll the others now."

She laughed. "I'm not so sure that'd be a good idea."

"It'll work out. It always does."

"Does it?" She felt unaccountably sad at her family's departure, at the decisions she had to make about her own situation.

"Yes."

"You all go down to the van," her mother told the others. "I want a minute alone with Cammy."

Camilla shot an accusatory look at Brandy who shrugged and mimed a zipper against her lips. "Not me," she mouthed.

After the elevator closed, her mother snapped her fingers. "Oh shoot. Your father had the key. We can't go back inside the room. Well, never mind. Come here."

She led Camilla into an alcove with an ice machine and said, "I want you to promise me you won't do anything rash."

Camilla kicked a stray piece of ice into the corner. "Why would you say that?"

"Because when people are in extreme situations of stress, life and death situations, it takes some time to get perspective when they come out of it."

"Mom—"

"Just listen to me, Cammy. I know you and the other girls think I'm too old to remember what it was like to be young and foolish, but sadly for you, you're going to find out you're never too old for that."

She smiled. "I don't think you're old, Mom."

"So let me say my piece then. You went through a scary, scary thing, and as a consequence, you might be making choices that you otherwise wouldn't have made. That's fine. Understandable. *Healthy* even."

She added in an undertone, kicking a stray piece of ice

under the machine herself, "Though your father would kill me if he knew I was saying that to you because I think we both know what I mean by that."

Camilla leaned back against the ice machine. "What are you trying to say?"

"Don't beat yourself up for anything that happened after the crash, but *please, please* don't jump into anything now. You're not thinking like yourself. You've gotten very close to pulling back that veil, and you're still not seeing too clearly."

No use pointing out she hadn't been seeing too clearly before the crash either. Not when it came to Mason.

"And even if the other person seems sincere, heck *is* sincere at the time, *he* might not be seeing too clearly, either." Her mother shook a finger at her. "Did you know Christy Brinkley married a guy she barely knew who she'd gotten into a helicopter accident with and they were divorced, fighting like fiends over custody of their baby, a year later? Did you know that?"

"Who's Christy Brinkley?"

She threw up her hands. "Oh, for heaven's sake!"

Camilla laughed and kissed her cheek, leading her back into the hallway and pushing the button for the elevator. "Don't worry, Mom. I'm not marrying anybody right now. It's just that with the *veil back*—" She paused. "Is that a poem or something?"

"You don't go to mass anymore, do you?"

Camilla hurried on. "I want to take some time while I'm seeing whatever it is I'm seeing to try to figure out what I really want to do."

The elevator arrived. "Well, I can't argue with that."

With a last hug, she got on the elevator. "Keep us posted about you coming home. I think that's a very good idea for you right now."

"Will do."

"Love you."

"Love you, too," she said to the closing doors.

If Brandy really hadn't said anything to their mother, she was a lot more perceptive than Camilla had thought. Or she and Mason were a lot more obvious.

When she returned to her suite, Mason's door was open, and he emerged as she put her card key into her own. His brand-new khakis and white oxford looked very out of place with the same beat up sneakers.

"Marcia works fast," she said as they went into her suite.

"She sent them over last night it turns out. They were at the front desk."

The bed where they'd made love all night was still rumpled, the sheets half on the floor, the comforter pushed to the bottom. She turned away from it.

"Your parents get off okay?"

"Fine."

"I'm sorry I didn't, ah, whatever," he said ambiguously, brushing her hair from her eyes, linking his arms around her waist.

She shrugged away. Time to bite the bullet. Fish or cut bait. Whatever. "I need some time."

He froze. "Time?"

"Yes, to think things over."

He dropped his eyes and stared at his shoes. "We're all set to take a charter back this morning. The pilots are standing by. London or New York, you say the word."

"I can't do that right now." Not just the plane, but everything, this sudden closeness with him, her intense feelings. Her mom was right. She didn't know if the gut wrenching ache in the pit of her stomach at the thought of being anywhere but in his arms was a real thing or if it was just an extreme reaction to life and death circumstances.

"All right, we'll stay here for a few days. I can put off the meeting. I'd rather be alone with you anyway."

"I don't think we should jump into that. Us, I mean. In fact, I might go home for a while. To Michigan."

"A…a vacation?" He stumbled over the word, like he'd never used it before.

But a short week away, then back in the boardroom and bedroom, wasn't what she was proposing. He couldn't be her boss *and* her lover. She had known that all along. The only question was whether he could still be even one of those. Whether they were really right for each other, as different as they were.

"No, not a vacation. I have some money saved, and if I live with my parents temporarily, my only expense will be my student loan payments. I can last for a while until I… I don't know. Decide what I want to do."

"Don't do this, Camilla." His voice was low and intense, the blue eyes focused on her now, not his sneakers. "Come back with me."

She shook her head, and he turned away quickly. "I thought we did all this last night. Settled all this."

"We settled that we feel something for each other, but not what we should do about it."

The curls on the back of his neck just brushed his collar, and she wished she could reach out to him. A pad of hotel stationary rested on the nearby desk, and he ripped off a sheet, then folded it in two. "I know what I want to do about it."

"I need time."

"Yes, you said that." The sheet was folded into quarters, then even smaller until it was a square that fit neatly in his palm. "How much time?"

"I don't know. I'm sorry."

He launched the wad of paper at the wastebasket but missed. "Is this because of what happened at breakfast? I'm not used to that kind of situation. If I did something wrong, I didn't mean to. It was the sperm thing, right?"

"No, you did fine," she lied. "You don't know my family, my brother. All breakfast did was remind me how different we are."

"I said I wanted to know them."

"Well, you didn't make a very good start this morning," she snapped.

He bent to retrieve the misfired paper and dropped it in safely.

"I'm sorry," she said in a rush. "I shouldn't have said that."

He glanced sideways at her. "And you're not going to give me a chance, are you?"

She was about to say it wasn't about her family, but that wasn't true. It was, partly anyway. The rest was about her and what she wanted out of life. Trite as it was, the plane crash had reminded her of her own mortality. If death came sooner than she expected, would she be content to say she had spent the last years of her life paying off her student loans and doing a profession she hated in a city that had never felt like home? There had to be some better way to figure out her future, and she needed some time, finally, to try to come up with one.

"What does that matter anyway?" he went on, his voice clipped. "I live in New York. You live in New York. How often would I even see your family? Do you see even them? When it was just us, it was fine."

She sighed, sitting in the chair by the bed. "It's not just us. We don't live in a hermetically sealed airplane all the time or on a deserted trail."

"A plane is not hermetically sealed," he muttered.

"You asked me why I hadn't been with anyone in so long. It was because I realized there wasn't any future in it with the guys I dated in the city. I don't want to be with a workaholic New Yorker who thinks that money is everything and who lives in a five hundred square foot box forty floors up. I want to be away from all that someday."

He stared at her. After a minute he said, "My apartment is a four-story townhouse on the upper east side. You could probably fit your parent's house in it three times over."

"It's not about money."

"What is it about then?" His face was flushed, and he jabbed his hands into the pockets of those nice new khakis. "You don't want me? Is that what you're saying here?"

She took a deep breath. He stood before her chair, close enough for her to reach out and touch the lean cheek she knew would be warm or circle one thick wrist and coax a long-fingered hand from a pocket. Bring the palm to her lips and place a gentle kiss there.

But she wasn't doing either of them any favors if she wasn't honest. "You're a wonderful guy. I never imagined when I walked into your office two days ago— God, was that only two days?"

He didn't smile, and she stumbled on.

"I never imagined how much I would enjoy being with you, like you…"

He said nothing.

"But I can't work for somebody I'm sleeping with, and I don't know what you're envisioning otherwise. I need to take a good look at my life right now, take this opportunity to think, since I'm out of a job and everything anyway."

She tried smiling again, but it faded away quickly. For once she didn't feel much like smiling. She got to the point.

"I can't just drop my career or what's left of it, with no other plans for the future but to be your girlfriend, if that's even what you're talking about. By your own admission, you've never even had one."

"You're not arguing a case here." His tone was sharp. "And I said I'd marry you."

"Mason! Come on. That's not realistic. We just met each other."

He turned away, moving back to the desk, passing up the pad of paper for a ballpoint pen, flicking it around on the surface pad with one finger until it toppled off the edge. He shoved his wayward hand back into his pants pocket again as if to stop any further nervous movements. "You hate being a lawyer. Why can't you give it up? And don't say the fucking loans," he hastened to add. "I can take care of those. You know that."

"I can't let you. That's not who I am."

He rounded on her. "Then come back to New York with me. Or we'll go to London. Take that meeting. You say you can't just drop your career, so don't drop it. *I* never asked you to. You're my lawyer. At least give that a chance. Try the job out. You worked in a firm before. How do you know you wouldn't love being in-house?"

"Believe me, even if I did, there's a rule against sleeping with the boss. You can't. I can't."

"I'll leave you alone. I won't try to, we don't have to—"

"That would never work."

"You're leaving without notice." He straightened, taking his hands out of his pockets to fold them across his chest, his stance wide and his tone unmistakably boss, not lover. "Even Shreeman stayed until I hired his replacement. I have ongoing deals continuously. You're going to quit on the spot? That's not very professional."

Her mouth thinned. "I think I've gone way beyond not being professional, don't you?"

"No. I don't. We've had one meeting and you did fine. I have a dozen more scheduled in the next few weeks. Stick with me before you disappear to do your thinking, at least until I can hire a new lawyer."

She let out a sigh, leaning back in the armchair. "Is this really necessary?"

"Yes. And then you can decide what to do. Take the time you want and we'll…see."

She rubbed her forehead. "We can't sleep together then. Not if you want me to stay on for two weeks or however long you need to hire someone. I mean it. That just does not work." When he made no response, she called his name.

"I heard you." He uncrossed his arms, one hand tangling in his hair as he glanced at the bed, and then went to the door. "The van is coming to take us and the pilots to the

Halifax airport in an hour. I'll meet you downstairs."

"Wait!" she said quickly, ignoring the softening of his features, as if he expected her to call him back to that bed. "I don't know if I can get on a plane right now."

He turned away. "It's statistically virtually impossible for us to get in a crash a day and a half after we almost got in one."

"Very comforting," she whispered when he was gone.

M ason didn't say a word to her when she got into the van, and though Boyd and Ray seemed to sense the more sober mood, they greeted her heartily, making jokes about getting on a plane again.

As they drove to Halifax, she commented, "It's bad enough to be a passenger again so soon, but I wouldn't think you'd want to get behind the wheel, or whatever the equivalent is in a plane right now. Don't you ever get a day off, to just chill and recover?"

"We're deadheading," Boyd said. She was beginning to be able to tell them apart. Though they had similar short, light hair and coloring and height, Boyd was a little older than Ray and had hazel eyes instead of green.

This morning neither of them were in uniform, sporting navy turtlenecks and the ubiquitous khakis. Marcia had texted her that their luggage would be transferred from the downed plane to the new one. So either Marcia had shopped for everyone but her, or they had gone to the mall themselves. She still wore Brandy's jeans and shirt. She'd change on the plane.

"Deadheading? What does that mean?"

"We're catching a ride with you to London. There are a slew of measures the FAA requires before we can take the controls again. There'll be other pilots handling this flight."

Lowering the newspaper he had been hiding behind since the ride began, Mason said, "Let's hope they do a better job of getting us to London than you two did."

Camilla blinked, then tried a laugh, though it came out forced. "He's kidding of course."

The pilots shrugged. "We hope they have more luck, too. Hell, we'll be on the plane, won't we?"

The newspaper was back up again.

Once at the new jet, disturbingly similar to the old jet, she retrieved her suitcase and changed in the restroom into a fresh pair of slacks, a sweater, and some new flats. When she came out, the pilots sat in one row of seats next to each other farther down the jet, chatting, and Mason was closer to the front in a window seat. Instead of taking the seat next to him, given his rude comment and silence, she assumed an aisle seat across from the pilots, smiling at them.

As the plane began to taxi and her stomach dropped, she regretted the distance between her and Mason. She supposed it was necessary if they were to get through the next few weeks in a business-like fashion.

Happily, the weather was calm and mild as they got to the cruising altitude, and she closed her eyes to try to sleep. God knew she hadn't gotten much the night before. Just the memory of what she had gotten, though, popped her eyes open. Maybe she should try a magazine. There was a rack of them by the restroom. After unbuckling her seatbelt, she headed there, not even glancing at Mason as she passed him, flipping through the offerings before she chose a Newsweek.

On her way back to her seat he called out, "Camilla."

Prepared for more bad manners, she almost melted when he said, "You okay? With the flight?"

She nodded. "I'll be fine. Thanks for asking."

He looked out his window. "Good. Good."

Feeling a little better, she found when she got back to her seat that she could sleep. Putting up the armrest, she snuggled on the sofa the two spacious seats created without it, her head toward the window. Slipping off her flats, palms beneath one cheek, she drifted off.

M ason stared at the clouds outside his window, his head pounding to the faint sound of the deadhead pilots chatting away. He wished he could tell fucking Boyd or Roy or whoever to shut up. He'd only offered them the ride when Camilla put down her conditions for staying until he could find her replacement. He thought their presence might help him to keep his hands off her. The way he was feeling, though, he might just stuff them in the closet and take the sleeping Camilla in his arms and kiss her awake.

But he couldn't. He had promised her. And she hadn't even admitted she would want him to. What the fuck did this "taking time" thing mean? Marcia finally consented to answer his phone calls but had placed an unsettling embargo on discussing his relationship with Camilla. So who else was he supposed to talk to about this? Talking to Camilla herself only left him even more confused. And, fuck, kind of hurt.

The way she was with him on the plane, eventually

anyway, and on the trail was one thing. And the way she had looked at him when he was covered in scrambled eggs and jam was another. And the way she spoke to him after breakfast, automatically assuming a distance he hadn't in a million years imagined she could erect so quickly, was even worse. He had thought they were starting something together, and it turned out not only was she not so sure, she was mulling over ending it. Or that was what it sounded like to him, and Marcia was zero help.

Never had he felt like such a…failure. Her family was so *loud*. Overwhelmingly loud and confusing. How could a handful of people dashing off comments to each other so quickly it was like a volleyball match at his prep school make him feel just as nervous as fifty lawyers and bankers swarming around him in a conference room?

As angry as he was at Camilla right now, he was just as lost about what to do about it and just as desperate that he should find something, anything that would keep her. He didn't give a fuck about her replacement or the deals he had on hold, including the one they were journeying to, but it was the only thing he could think of to keep her from disappearing from his life, as he had a sneaking suspicion this "thinking" thing would result in her doing. And he was very sorry he hadn't realized that the "not sleeping with her" rule would come along with her remaining on the job. But if that was the only way she would stay with him for now, he could handle it.

Or he thought he could. Until he saw her smiling at the pilots, at *them*, like she should have been smiling at him.

Fuck, this should be one interesting couple weeks, but at least he would have time to figure out what to do. Because one thing he knew, he did not want to let her go. Being with her had been the only time in his life where he had felt at home in his skin. Where he didn't mind whoever he was, different as that may be, and he didn't want to lose that sensation. He didn't want to lose her.

He fingered the pearls still in his jacket pocket.

Was it wrong of him to wish the plane would crash again?

# Chapter Ten

They landed in London, and she checked into her hotel while Mason went to his apartment. He didn't press her to stay overnight with him, and she appreciated it.

Maybe, just maybe, some crazy version of this arrangement *could* work.

The next morning she met him at the solicitor's office, less flashy than Bannum and Strauss or any of the other New York law firms, no two-story lobby or winding staircase, only a small reception room. They were both early and told it would be a few minutes. The conference room they were led to was all polished oak and built-in bookcases and a gray marble table that would seat a dozen or so.

Mason fidgeted with some papers he'd brought relating to the proposed deal. He hadn't looked at her since they met in the lobby. Dressed in fresh clothes, he was still considerably underdressed, jeans and a T-shirt, no slogan on it this time, just pure Florida orange juice bright, with yet another hideous jacket, green wool, to complete the outfit.

"You're not color blind, are you?" she asked in an aside.

"No. Why do you ask?" He finally looked at her, and as ever, those big blue eyes, long black lashes captivated her.

She smiled. "No reason."

The solicitor came in after a short awkward silence and introduced himself as Nigel Bennett. His client arrived a minute or two after that. Given the preliminary nature of the meeting, she had only skimmed the file, a million years ago by now. She pulled it out of her computer bag to glance at it again. Just as she had thought. Despite that the principal whose company Talbot, Inc. was interested in acquiring looked like a male model for Italian cologne, Lorenzo Mancusa was actually CEO of a struggling fiber optics operation in Venice.

When Camilla introduced herself and shook his hand, he held it a minute too long, his chocolate brown eyes staring steadily at her, his accent fluid and light. "*So* pleased to meet you, Miss Anderson."

Unlike Mason's messy curls and classic bone structure, this man's perfectly blown-dried brown hair, tanned smooth skin, and manicured nails did nothing to start her pulse racing. She could never be with a man who just might be prettier than she was. Besides, she was with—

She stopped herself. Was she with Mason? Wasn't she? It was hard to tell. She was positive whatever bargain they had struck was just temporary. It would blow up in their faces soon enough. Then she'd have to make some real decisions.

She glanced sideways to catch Mason glaring at her for some reason. After the silence this morning and then that look, maybe it would blow up even sooner.

Mr. Mancusa wandered over to the sidebar for coffee and Danish alongside blue and white patterned china. Camilla rose to refill her cup, and he leaned toward her, close, and asked in a tone too smooth to be businesslike, "Can I *interest* you in *something*?"

His speech was full of italics.

Was she giving off pheromones or something?

She smiled, which was something she was starting to think she did way, way too much, especially in a business context. But when she tried to stop herself, her lips hovered over her teeth like horses at the racetrack, not a very attractive image let alone sensation, and if she was able to refrain from it, she ended up feeling like a bitch. It was easier to go with her natural instincts and smile. "No. No, thanks. I'm getting some coffee here. Would you like coffee, Mason?"

He shook his head.

When they all sat at the table, Nigel summarized the proposed deal structure succinctly as Lorenzo gave her the eye, starting at her lips, smiling of course, then down to her neck and the beginnings of her collarless shirt. And farther down still. She hunched slightly. No, she was not imagining this. She'd been to Italy for business and knew Italian men's boundaries were even more porous than Mason's had been on the plane, but she did not need this right now. Especially since Mason caught her eye several times, glaring, as if he somehow blamed her for Mancusa checking her out.

A side of her lip went up, and she rolled her eyes, trying to indicate how ridiculous she thought this in-person stereotype of the Latin lover was behaving, but Mason gave no indication he understood.

At least the meeting itself chugged along just fine.

Whereas in the gathering in New York, Mason did not participate or even appear to be listening, in this smaller group, he snapped out questions about production quotas and supply bases with regularity throughout the other side's presentation, consulting his papers, writing actual notes, not doodles, following the train of thought of the answers and coming back with even more pressing inquiries. He clearly knew his own business, but whether Lorenzo could say the same was iffy.

After a series of particularly grueling back and forths, Mason said, "I need a few minutes to consult with my counsel."

Lorenzo and Nigel stood up. Lorenzo wiped his brow. "Make no mistake, Mr. Talbot," he said. "You brought this deal to me. I can take it or leave it."

Camilla glanced at the income statement Mason had handed her earlier in the meeting. "Not with the way your enterprise is leaking cash. You need a company like Talbot behind you to staunch some of that until you can stabilize your supply base."

Lorenzo clicked his tongue. "Barbs along with such beauty. Makes it more interesting, does it not, Mr. Talbot?"

"What the fuck is that supposed to mean?" Mason shot back.

Nigel interceded. "I think we all need some time to cool off so we can approach this in a more constructive manner. Miss Anderson, we'll give you and your client a few minutes to discuss how you want to proceed."

"Thank you."

When the door shut behind them, Camilla said, "*Do* you want this company? It looks shaky to me. If you end up deciding to enter into a contract, I'd advise it be conditioned on the due diligence to make sure nothing really ugly comes up. I didn't like Mancuso. He seems slimy."

"Is that right? He obviously liked you just fine." Now that they were alone, he was absorbed in his papers again.

She rubbed her eyes, hoping at the last minute she hadn't smudged the little mascara she had on. "Italian men are all like that. Sorry for the generalization but it's pretty much true."

"Is it? You've known a lot of them, have you?"

She laughed. "You're not seriously—"

"I'm seriously commenting that the guy was fucking you with his eyes."

"You're being ridiculous."

He sat back in his chair, meeting her eyes, his own narrowed. "If I keep my hands off you, how does this work? Am I going to have to see other guys looking down your blouse in the meantime?"

"Where the hell is this coming from?" she demanded. "Where do you get off talking to me like that?"

When she had agreed to stay on until replaced, she hadn't meant he could ignore her as he seemed to being doing earlier or berate her as he was doing now.

"This is not okay, Mason."

His cheeks were flushed, his jaw set. "I'm getting fucking sick of all these rules about what's okay and what's not okay."

She stood up and he tugged her down, leaning toward her, whispering, "*Where is this coming from? Where is this coming from?* I'll tell you where. Last night, I spent the first night without you since I met you and I didn't like it. I wanted you beside me, to snuggle with you and watch you while you sleep. To wake up with me and talk to me—"

He took a deep breath, appearing to try to calm himself, and she ran her eyes over his face, shocked by all this emotion, but touched by it at the same time. She had spent a sleepless night herself last night. "Mason..."

"And then I have to sit here and watch that asshole flirt with you. Know that it's okay for him to be with you because he's not your boss. Isn't that right?"

"No," she rasped. "That isn't right. For one thing, he's on the other side. Conflict of interest."

"How reassuring."

A loud knock and Nigel came back in as Mason and Camilla automatically leaned away from each other. Lorenzo followed and they sat back down.

"Excuse me for intruding so soon. But as Lorenzo and I were discussing this briefly on our own, the possibility of lowering the range of acceptable purchase prices arose. It might be more constructive to frame our discussion around that for the purposes of this meeting and leave further due diligence questions for once the contract is signed."

"Only if the contract has an out in it for anything we find unacceptable in the due diligence phase," she insisted.

"Anything? That's rather wide, my dear Miss Anderson," Mancusa said with another trip of his eyes down her blouse. "Wide enough to shove something very *big* right through."

*What?* she almost said. As an argument, that didn't even make much sense. If there was a big problem discovered in the diligence, of course they would take the out. He undoubtedly meant that something *small* could slip through and be counted as an out. But that didn't fit with what she gathered was supposed to be a lame penis metaphor. Maybe it worked better in Italian.

"We don't know what we don't know," she settled on. It was one of the more confusing legal truisms, but she liked throwing that one around sometimes.

"Granted," Nigel admitted. "Let's concede that we will negotiate the conditions to closing with an open mind on your concern there."

Mason flipped through his notes. "I'm not signing any contract at all until I decide whether it's even worth my trouble."

Lorenzo sat back in a huff. "There's been turbulence in the supply base. Fine. I admit it."

"Your financials *admit* it," Mason said. "And these aren't even audited. God knows what an audit will turn up."

"Are there foibles in this business as there are in any?" Nigel asked, holding his hands up, palms out. "Of course there are. But with your astute management team, I feel confident you'll be equal to them, Mr. Talbot. Now about that purchase price range."

But Mason would not be put off of further questions. He continued with them, sharp, on point, until Lorenzo finally said, with exasperation, "Please, Mr. Talbot. Won't you and your lovely attorney come to my home, see my plant in our beautiful Venice, and then decide for yourself whether it is *worth your time,* as you say? We could be there in hours rather than haggling over insignificant matters at a stuffy conference table in," he looked around as if not sure where he was, since it was so nondescript in comparison to Venice, "London."

Mason sat back. "*Me* and Miss Anderson? Wouldn't you

like it to be just Miss Anderson? Wouldn't that be much better?"

The aggression in his tone caused Lorenzo to tilt his head, staring from Mason to her and then back again, ending with a smirk for Mason as he finally understood the undercurrents and a look for Camilla that made his previous facial dalliances tame by comparison, eyebrows raised and nod employed along with a knowing look.

She flushed despite not wanting to. Only upside was she didn't feel like smiling. She dropped her gaze.

"Ah, you *are* a lucky man, Mr. Talbot."

She pursed her lips, and Nigel, as a Brit, probably not even understanding the undercurrents, said, "If you don't feel it's necessary to go on a plant tour at this time, Mr. Talbot, you certainly are free to make that decision, but if your attorney goes, I will have to accompany my client."

"Lorenzo wouldn't want you there, Nigel, any more than he'd want me there, right, Lorenzo?" Mason asked.

The other man shrugged.

"All right, that's enough," she said quietly, sticking to the point. They could pull their dicks out and piss to mark their territory later. "It's premature to take a plant tour or even discuss one. I need a moment alone with my client, please, for us to, ah, finish the discussion we were having. And I assure you we *will* discuss purchase price if it's merited, all right?"

Lorenzo, still smiling, sauntered out, Nigel closing the door behind him.

When they were alone again, she turned on him. "That whole exchange was getting ridiculous. Is this how you plan to conduct yourself for the duration of my employment?

Because I'm not finding it very promising."

"What about you? Is this how you plan to act?" he fired back.

"Yes. I've done absolutely nothing unprofessional in this meeting. You're the one who's practically sending up smoke signals to that sleazy guy that we're fucking. Get a grip."

He grabbed her arms, leaning into her. A grip all right. She had forgotten how literal he was.

"No, I mean—"

"I know what you mean. Tell me you'd never consider being with him, somebody like him. Or somebody like Nigel, or fuck, anybody!"

She stared at him and he loosened his hold.

Dusting her knuckles against the hollow of his cheek, she thought how beautiful he was, how real, despite all his faults, or maybe because of them. Nothing like the sleek image of a man that Lorenzo seemed to be trying so hard to project. "No, I don't want anyone but you. That's the truth."

He held her face in his hands, tucked a stray hair behind her ear. They were within inches of each other, so close she could feel his breath. Almost close enough to kiss. He looked at her lips and ran one thumb softly against them. "Then whatever you do, don't turn me away, Camilla."

She was the one who moved closer. Her lips crushed against his, her pulse beating wildly, and her tongue sought his.

With a groan, he cupped the back of her neck, bringing her further into the kiss, yanking the clip that secured her hair so it came tumbling down around them, his other hand busy caressing her throat, and then her breasts through the silk of her blouse, each sweep of his hand setting her on fire.

They moved to standing as one, and he thrust his leg between hers, as much as her skirt would allow, causing a sensation as evocative as if he'd entered her, his erection, heavy and substantial, prodding her between her legs.

"I want you," he murmured, bending her backward toward the table as they kissed.

As hot as that simple statement made her, she had not forgotten where they were.

"I don't think…" she tried to get out.

But through the haze of pleasure, he positioned her until the marble table was level with her bottom and then hiked up her skirt, the rasp of his hands urgent.

*Oh, Jesus.*

He was drugging her with long, deep kisses that felt as if they were reaching into her heart. He managed to place his hands on her everywhere at once, fondling her sensitive breasts until her nipples were aching, yanking down her panties to her thighs so she was bare to his caresses. He divested her of her suit jacket and top, the collarless stretchy cotton not much of an impediment to him, shoving it up, and pushed aside the cups of her bra to place his hot lips on one nipple, teasing with his tongue, and then the other, licking, sucking.

She groaned at the onslaught of pleasure, the rush of it so unexpected, so inappropriate. "We can't…we shouldn't… Mason, no." Her voice got firmer. "Not here."

She put a palm to his chest, pushing lightly, and it was enough to back him away, as if he finally came to himself. Straightening, he ran a hand through his hair. "You're right. I'm sorry."

He turned his back on her, probably conjugating those

Greek verbs again, as she straightened her clothes.

There was a throat clearing out in the hallway, loud enough to announce someone's presence, and a knock on the door.

"Give us a minute," Mason barked, and Camilla rolled her eyes.

"Let's just get through with the meeting for now without giving Lorenzo any more hints about our relationship."

"I don't give a fuck. I hope that asshole sees you're mine."

"You certainly did your best," she said softly.

"And I'm not buying his shitty company. Not because he wants to fuck you—"

"I doubt he even does. It's just his style."

"But because it's a shitty company."

"Okay." She unzipped her computer case and stuffed her papers back in. "Deal's dead then. That'll make the meeting take considerably less time."

She opened the door to Lorenzo's sly smile and Nigel's blush.

It ended up taking a bit longer than she thought it would, the other side arguing their case and lowering their price so quickly and repeatedly that she had no doubt the due diligence would have shown something even more disastrous than the financials had. But Mason behaved himself, regaining his cool and letting her deliver the "no." They all shook hands at the end, and Nigel and Lorenzo left, whispering of alternatives before the conference door even closed on them.

She stood up and Mason followed suit.

"So I guess we should fly back to New York," he said tentatively.

She bit her lip, shaking her head.

"I was out of line. I know I was. I'm sorry."

"We shouldn't have this conversation here. It's too private. Someone might walk in."

"Come back with me to my apartment."

"No! I need to... I need some space to..."

He stared at her for a second and then locked the conference door. "Fine. Say it. Whatever you're going to say. I deserve it."

He looked so contrite that for a second she lost the words. Just lost them. The ones that were going to make all the reasonable arguments about why this wouldn't work, the two of them attending meetings together and pretending they were not...whatever they were to each other.

She put a hand on his shoulder and took a step closer, feeling a rush of tenderness toward him as he brought it to his lips, palm up.

One gentle kiss, his warm mouth against her skin, and what had been banked earlier burst into full conflagration, as if the locked door had unleashed something wild in them.

Suddenly, there were only hungry kisses and urgent caresses. She yanked up his shirt to mold his hot flesh, and he lifted her skirt and slid her panties down until it was her naked bottom against the marble now as he pushed her down, cool and erotic. With a deft touch between her legs, he confirmed she was wet and ready. Shocking her, he brought his finger up, rubbing the moistness against her tender lips swollen from his kisses, dipping it into her mouth.

"Taste how much you want me." He undid his pants with shaking hands, taking his cock out so the scorching heat of him pressed against her bare thigh. "Feel how much I want you."

She moaned.

"Say you want me, Camilla," he urged, his voice low, hoarse. "Say it."

"I want you," she whispered between kisses. "God, of course I want you."

Without warning, he flipped her over, her palms bracing on the table to keep from slamming against it. "Then take me. Please, Camilla," he muttered. "*Now*."

And he shoved his cock inside her, throbbing, hard and deep, and so very right.

With one hand tangled in her hair, the other clutched her hip convulsively as he moved her in rhythm to his wild thrusts, each one accompanied by a low groan, the sound and feel of him slapping against her naked bottom as he fucked her making her wetter, more desperate.

It all was so hot. Her partial nudity while he was still as good as clothed, the hoarse cries he uttered, burying himself deeper and deeper until she could hardly breathe.

She didn't realize she was making loud, satisfied noises, until he soothed "shhh" and she tried to hold it in. But at one particularly deep thrust, he cried out so loudly, "Fuck!" that she thought surely someone would hear them.

And still he kept on, as they both panted and strained to the incredible symphony of them moving against each other.

"I want this," he got out between his teeth, "every time I look at you…every time I touch you…oh, God…every time you smile—"

He came, shuddering against her, and the spasms of his cock pushed her to climax as well.

The cool marble against her cheek registered just as she remembered where they were.

Her panties were around her thighs, her engorged nipples against the table and her skirt hiked up as high as it would go.

"Shit." Some paragon of feminism she was turning out to be. *Could she make it through one work day without getting seduced into fucking him please?*

Still panting, he pulled out of her slowly, retrieving a napkin from the sideboard and cleaning himself off before he zipped his pants.

She did the same, wiping between her legs, and straightened her clothes. The smell of sex permeated the air, and they didn't meet each other's eyes.

"I meant for us to talk when I locked the door," he finally said softly. "I did. I didn't mean for us to—"

"I know. With us, it just…happens." He seemed to tense, zipping his briefcase, as if waiting for the "but."

She was shaken by how quickly, how heedlessly it had *happened*, in a conference room, in the middle of the business day, with an entire law firm only one wooden door away. Her emotions and actions when she was with him seemed increasingly at odds with her words, with what she knew was the right thing to do for now. Her head was waging a powerful war with her heart. She needed to get a hold of herself, of both of them, no matter how much it was going to hurt.

"But for that very reason, this isn't going to work, me staying in this job. I knew it and we just proved it. I resign,

Mason. Effective immediately."

He nodded. "This whole meeting was a trap, wasn't it?"

"What?"

"I made a jealous ass out of myself and then you kissed me and I, I lost control. Not once, but *twice.*"

As ridiculous as all this was, fucking on a conference room table—geez, she hoped they cleaned it pretty thoroughly at night—without protection no less, *again,* she liked the way he said that. *He lost control.* But she couldn't let him take all the blame.

"It wasn't a trap. And we both lost control, for the record. I wanted it. I'm not denying that. I want you."

"Then stay with me."

She shook her head. "I need some time alone, and I don't want you to try to convince me otherwise this time. Okay?"

"Three days?" he suggested.

She placed a palm on his hot cheek. "Let me get myself together and we'll see. We need time, both of us, Mason, to get some perspective."

"How long?" he persisted.

She kissed him lightly. "As long as it takes."

Like so much of her life now, she had to take a step back and go from there.

# Chapter Eleven

Twenty-nine days. Mason could name the hours, but he didn't want to seem obsessive. It had been almost a full month since Camilla had walked out of that London office and out of his life, and he'd been a wreck ever since.

"This is not the fucking file I wanted!" he shouted at Marcia.

Ignoring him, she continued typing on her computer.

"Are you listening to me?"

"No, I'm not."

He stopped, shifting from foot to foot. "You just answered me, so you are, right?"

"Don't try to blind me with your stunning intelligence, boy."

"It's not the right file." He dropped the manila folder on her desk, sullen about it but at least quiet.

"Why should I give you the right file when we both know you won't be reading it? You'll just be staring out into space with that hangdog look on your face."

He ignored the hangdog comment. "I *was* reading it. How else would I know it was the wrong one?"

"There you go, putting a poor little secretary like me in my place with your high IQ."

"Poor little secretary, my ass," he muttered. "Can I have the right file please?"

She stopped typing and walked over to the door to the outer hallway, picking up his jacket from the coat rack on the way, and stood there, holding it out to him. "No, you cannot have the right file. You are going to go home and turn on the TV—"

"I don't have a TV."

"Yes, you do. You know that mammoth dark screen in your living room? It makes pretty pictures and sounds when you use that little remote thing to turn it on. So you are going to go home and turn it on and watch some mindless sitcom or rerun or whatever and just *relax*. You're driving me absolutely insane."

He tugged her out of the doorway, then slammed it shut. "I'm driving myself insane, too."

Collapsing on the couch in the waiting room, elbows on knees, he rested his head in his hands, registering the weight of it as pounds too heavy since he'd last seen Camilla.

"I'm sorry I ever even hired that girl," Marcia said with an edge to her voice that approached the one she had when she discussed his mother. She sat beside him on the couch. "But I did and you just have to put it behind you, Mason."

"She doesn't want me." There. He said it and was finally coming to understand, without one word from her since she had walked away from him, that it was true. And the world wasn't going to end because of it. It was only going to be a pale imitation of what it had been in the three or so days he'd spent with her.

"If she doesn't want you, then she's a hell of a lot dumber than I gave her credit for being."

"She doesn't care about my money."

"I'm not talking about your money!" She tipped his chin up, and he jerked it away, not looking at her.

"You are such a wonderful boy, Mason."

He had to smile, just a little, at the "boy." He'd always be a boy to Marcia. "I'm a nut, odd...awkward."

"Now, that's your mother talking."

"That's Camilla talking."

She shot up from the couch. "Did that girl have the goddamn nerve to say that to you? I'm going to call her up and give her such a piece of my mind!"

He pulled her back down. "No, of course she didn't say that. She's... *She's* wonderful."

"Not in my book, she 'aint."

The outer door opened and a man, dressed in neatly pressed trousers and a plaid shirt, started to enter, a roll of plans under his arm. Upon seeing the both of them sitting there, he backed out instead.

"No, that's okay Frank," he said. "Come on in. What do you have there?"

"I don't want to bother you, Mr. Talbot. I was just fixing to leave this and set up an appointment with Miss White here to maybe talk to you about them, whenever you get a moment."

"I have a moment now." He held his hand out, but Marcia swiped the roll away before he could take it.

"No, he doesn't," she said. "Sorry. But I'll check your calendar and set something up next week, how's that?"

"Oh, fine, just fine." The poor guy practically sprinted out.

"Give me those," Mason said to Marcia when the door closed behind him.

"No. You can look at them tomorrow or whenever."

"You didn't need to chase him out like that."

"See, like that. Like Frank."

"What about him?"

"You think most folks in your position would take somebody like him in, put him in the training program, somebody who I happen to know hasn't had an address for the last year or so, and give him a chance? Hell no!"

He shrugged. "The guy's a natural. I bet I'm going to look at those plans and be impressed."

"And I bet if you aren't, you're going to give him another chance and work with him. Don't think I don't know you made sure he got some help at AA."

"You don't have to do everything for me, Marcia. I can make a call on my own once and a while."

"Well, don't get used to it," she snapped. "Anyway, I'm just trying to say you're a good person, and if Miss High and Mighty doesn't see it, then she isn't."

He rested his head against the back of the couch. "Thanks. But she is a good person. I think she just... I don't know. I don't know anything."

"Have you called her?"

"I thought you wouldn't discuss specifics about me and her?"

"I can discuss a phone call. So the answer is probably

no, right?"

He shook his head, feeling lost and anxious as always at the thought of Camilla. And he'd thought of her a lot this past month. Kind of with every waking breath…and sleeping, too, since he dreamed about her—long, silky dreams where they touched and talked and laughed. Some where she just smiled. Even some where she actually had all her clothes on. "She asked me to give her time. Wouldn't calling her be reneging on that? Though, fuck, I've picked up the phone a dozen times."

"Which means a hundred times."

"Hundred and fifty, tops."

They smiled at each other.

"So you're really going through with this tonight? The whole burrito?"

He stood up. "I am. Time for me to get out into the real world, I guess."

He added, heading back to his own office, "Though I have no idea what that expression you just used means."


Camilla continued boxing up the contents of her studio apartment as her sister Carly sipped a Diet Coke and watched the proceedings.

"You can help here, you know? If you want to," Camilla said.

"I wouldn't dream of it. I'm sure you have a neat little system going on there, marking all the boxes so when you get them out of Mom and Dad's basement someday you'll know what they are. I don't do packing anyway. There are people for that."

"Yes, people like me."

"Besides, I object strenuously to this whole plan of yours. I think it's crazy."

Camilla placed her Blackstone's Law Dictionary in a box and, thinking better of it, tossed it into the trash. "Like you've never done anything crazy, sister dear."

Carly laughed, automatically bringing one finger up to the side of her mouth, perfectly outlined in red lipstick, smoothing any incipient lines that might have the nerve to try to appear. Unlike the extra weight Brandy sported, Carly kept rigid control over her sleek body, weighing the same as she had when she was twenty. She kept the same control over her exceedingly pretty face, only God and her dermatologist knew how. Camilla swore Carly looked younger than she did, though there were seven years between them, and Carly was on the wrong end of that, which no one would ever guess looking at the two of them together.

"Well you have me there," her sister admitted with a titter. "I have had a few *escapades* in my time." She sobered. "But this doesn't sound like an escapade so much as a recipe for poverty."

"It's what I want to do."

Carly consented to folding a suit jacket and placing it gingerly in a box other than the one with the matching skirt. Maybe she shouldn't help. "If it's what you want, then you should do it. Follow your dream and all that. It's just," she gave up on the packing and went to get another Diet Coke, "your dream is so boring!"

Unscrewing the icy bottle, Carly added, "Now my dream, if I were you, would be to marry the billionaire."

"Carly!"

"Seriously. Why not? I've had six thousand conversations with you in the last few weeks, ever since you got back from Michigan, where you've cried on my shoulder—"

"I never cried."

"You know what I mean. *Figuratively* cried on my shoulder about how much you cared for this guy, but you weren't sure he did for you."

"I think he probably doesn't know what he feels, and when I go back to his office, he'll have trouble remembering my name."

"Which is why I wasn't in favor of this time apart to 'think it over' thing in the first place. You had him where you wanted him."

Her sister shook her head with a smile. "You know I'm kidding. You did the right thing, and now you've figured out the rest of your life—news flash, you're going to be poor—you'll see how it turns out with the dreamy boss, right?"

"Right," she said, her stomach flipping with nervousness and excitement at the thought of all the plans she had ahead of her, not the least of which included seeing Mason again. She had missed him. If she had worried that her infatuation with him was temporary, the ache she felt these past weeks at not seeing him or talking to him had cured her of that. Illogical or not, the three days she had spent with him meant more to her than the previous five years or so. Ten probably. And if the same wasn't true for him, then her heart might just break, but if anything it would mean she was right about their enforced separation. "And he's my ex-boss."

"I only came over because I wanted to wish you luck." Her sister surveyed the half-filled boxes and bubble wrapped kitchen appliances. "I didn't know you'd be *working*. Shopping anyone?"

Camilla had timed her visit so it would be later in the day, well after five, in order to have less chance of running into anyone she knew at Talbot, Inc. on her way up to Mason's office. Probably the few who would even recognize her couldn't put a name to her face any more, since her tenure had been so brief. Mason included.

She stood outside the doors to the CEO's office suite for a good five minutes, before she got up the nerve to push through that door.

When she did, Marcia looked up from her computer. "Hello, Miss Anderson."

The coolness in the woman's voice stung Camilla, but she shouldn't have been surprised. She had not made Marcia's billionaire boss change for the better after all. She imagined she might have even made him worse. He was probably propositioning female employees left and right now.

"I was surprised when the guard in the lobby called," the assistant continued. "What can I do for you? Come to finally clean out your office?"

Despite how uncomfortable this was, she had to forge ahead. "I came to drop in on Mason, if that's okay."

The inner office was very quiet. If he was in there, and wasn't coming out at the sound of her voice, she had her answer.

She took a shaky breath.

"He's not here."

"Oh!" The rush of relief that flowed through her was childish. She couldn't put this off forever. She didn't want to keep postponing her life. "Maybe I could, ah… I mean, is he in town?"

"Depends."

As curt as Marcia was being, Camilla suddenly remembered that, Mason aside, she owed this woman a courtesy, should have even sent a note probably. "I wanted to thank you, by the way, on behalf of my family."

A pause. "For what?"

"For the generous donation to Special Friends." The chairman of the group wasn't supposed to divulge that the anonymous gift was given in her brother's name, but he was a family friend by now, and so he did, delighted by it. And there was only one person even remotely connected to Joey with five million dollars to donate to charity.

"What's Special Friends?" Marcia asked.

Camilla cocked her head. "It's a charity that, ah, offers some really wonderful services for my brother and men and women like him. You gave a donation to it. An incredibly generous one."

"I did not."

"It was anonymous, Marcia, but I know it was you. Or rather you did it on behalf of Mason. You probably did all the legwork, though, found out my brother's affiliation with it, and sent in the donation, so I wanted to thank you. And him of course. Mason. It was very thoughtful, especially given the circumstances."

Marcia went back to her typing. "It was thoughtful all right, hon, but I did no such thing."

"What?"

"You're right. If Mason had wanted to make a donation, I would have handled it, the man barely knows how to write a check these days, but I've never heard of Special Friends."

She tilted her head. "You're kidding."

The typing stopped. "God's truth. Though it sounds sort of like Camp for Kids, which Mason started actually and is still very supportive of."

"What?" This was all not computing.

Marcia got up from her desk and showed Camilla to the couch. She must look worse than she thought she did for the woman to soften up and offer her a seat. They sat down, a few feet away from each other. "The charity you mentioned, Special Friends. It sounds like Mason's charity. Camp for Kids is devoted to getting special children and teens who live in cities out to the country for a few weeks. You'd be amazed at what a kick these kids get out of the horses and the hay rides."

"Camp for Kids is for..." She hesitated, since in her family there were no other words for what Joey was, and certainly none of the words that used to be so common. Not even handicapped. He wasn't handicapped. "*Special* kids? That's what Mason's been donating to, before he met me, you mean."

Marcia crossed her arms over her substantial chest before she then pointed one finger at Camilla, shaking it. "Let me tell you something, missy, Mason is just about the most good-hearted person I know, and he *was* way before you showed up to kick him in the balls."

Ouch. "I didn't—"

"Since you came in here, and didn't even have the good manners to otherwise inform me you were leaving, I'm going to tell you just what I think of how you treated that poor boy. He mopes around here all day and can't even concentrate on his work and he went out yesterday and got himself a damn cat, and who do you bet is going to have to change the litter!"

She laughed. "Mason got a cat?"

"For your information, yes he did. Now I've known Mason since he was a little baby and that nutty mama of his acted like she cooked him up in a test tube and wanted to throw the batch back and start mixing ingredients again. Thank God she had to get a hysterectomy after she had him or she'd have been torturing some other kid now."

"Torturing?" she said in alarm.

"It's a turn of phrase. You're getting as literal minded as he is." She rose to retrieve a bottle of water from the fridge by her desk and tossed one to Camilla without asking. "Now, where was I?"

Camilla took a deep breath and a sip of the water. It looked like this was going to be a more lengthy conversation with Marcia than the quick exercise in good manners she'd envisioned.

"I thought you were her friend. His mother's, I mean."

"You think I wanted to stay 'friends' with Mason's mama, Rita? Friends, hell! I only did it for the boy, the cutest little thing I ever saw, all black curls and blue eyes, Rita complaining that he didn't talk for so long and didn't want to be held. Who'd want that harpy holding him?"

"Ah, so not a friend."

"More like a defensive tackle these days, just trying to keep her out of his life. And then *you* come along."

She held up one hand. "Stop. Wait. I don't know what he

told you—"

"Damn near nothing since he got back from London and you didn't. For a week I thought you were still there negotiating the deal, for God's sake. And now, he barely says a word to anyone unless he's snapping it."

"I'm sorry."

"Not me you should be saying that to. Now I don't know about that charity thing you mentioned, if that's all you wanted, but I think you got more business with Mason than that if you don't mind me saying."

She nodded. No reason to hide it. In fact, it was looking up on that score, though there were still some unanswered questions. "Has Mason gone to any PR parties since he got back?"

"Parties! Girl, have you been listening to a word I've said?"

"I have, and thank you." She patted her hand. "And as to Special Friends, I think I know what happened. I think Mason donated that money to my brother's charity."

"I just told you he didn't."

"No, I think *he* did. On his own. Anonymous and not even through you because he didn't want anybody to know."

"Honey, I hate to burst your bubble, but I don't think Mason's capable of that, the mechanics I mean."

She stood up. "I think Mason's capable of a lot more than you, or *I* give him credit for."

"Well, I'll ask him."

"No! No, you don't. I'll ask him. Is he in town?"

A long pause indicated Marcia was on the fence as to whether to let Camilla into her boss's life again. Finally, she said, "He is in town. And you might be interested to know where he'll be tonight."

Mason didn't trust himself to pick up his wineglass his hand was shaking so badly. There were a dozen people sitting on the dais in the ballroom, and as if the whole setup wasn't bad enough, they had insisted he assume his place up there with them. So now the entire audience at tables on the main floor, one hundred and twenty guests, all the women in their long, glittery dresses and jewels and men in their tuxedoes, had paid five hundred a ticket to see that he could barely touch his chicken dinner. They could probably hear his stomach growling as well, not from hunger but from nerves. Every pulse in his body urged him to flee, but he remained rooted to his seat.

The young man next to him, barely out of his teens if he had to guess, reached over and scooped up a French fry from Mason's plate and popped it into his own mouth with a big grin. Dressed in a tuxedo, too, his neighbor looked infinitely more comfortable in the evening wear than Mason did, not even bothering about the dollop of ketchup he had dropped on his lapel, though his outfit probably fit him about the same as Mason's, too short in the sleeves and loose in the waist. Mason tried to remember the guy's name as the woman on the other side of him leaned over and said, "Nathan, you know that's not polite. That's Mr. Talbot's plate."

Nathan. That was it.

"Don't worry about it. I'm not hungry right now."

"Can I have all your French fries then?"

"Nathan," the woman remonstrated. Mason couldn't

remember her name, either, but he was pretty sure she was on the board.

He pushed the plate toward Nathan. "Go for it."

The young man dug in, his own plate clean. Between bites, he said, "Why aren't you hungry?"

Mason yanked on his bowtie. The board member had turned away to the woman on the other side of her, and he leaned a little toward his co-conspirator. "I'm nervous."

"You are?" Nathan started in on the chicken, picking the lightly basted piece up in his hands. Mason was glad the board member had turned away. He for one thought hands were the only way a person should eat chicken, but not everyone agreed. The woman on the other side of Nathan had already insisted he use a fork on his own chicken breast.

"Why are you nervous?" he asked. "Because you have to sit up here? I'm not nervous. They said it was because I was so good that I got to sit up here, next to you even."

Mason smiled. "Next to me, huh? What's so special about me?"

Nathan paused, his fingers buttery from the chicken, and Mason handed over a napkin, which he took and put the chicken down, wiping his mouth and his fingers. "I don't know what's so good about you, but they said you were the guest of honor."

"Apparently."

"Don't be nervous."

"I'll try, but I'm supposed to give a speech."

"Me, too!" he confided with a grin even wider than when he'd been snatching a French fry. "But I'm not nervous at all."

"You're a better man than I am, Nathan."

"I don't think so. But thank you."

Mason smiled. "You're welcome."

The woman board member stood up and went to the podium in the center of the dais, then tapped on the microphone that he had been distressed to see was there.

"Now, ladies and gentleman, we've let you eat long enough. It's time for the actual ceremony part. We are so lucky to have with us tonight a man who has given so much of himself to Camp for Kids."

"That's you," Nathan stage whispered.

"I guess." He barely got the words out.

"And tonight he's giving us something even more precious, a little of his very valuable time to meet some of you and let us thank him properly for his contributions." Someone handed her a plaque. "Mr. Talbot." She waved him over.

"You better go," Nathan said, very loud, and the audience laughed. Softer, he added, "Don't be scared."

Mason nodded and went up to the microphone.

She handed him the plaque as the audience clapped. His face flushed under the bright lights, and his breathing sounded very loud to him in the microphone. After a minute, the board member faded back, resuming her seat, and he was up there, alone, the only noise some rustling of chairs as people positioned themselves to listen to him.

He set the plaque down on the table and reached into his inner pocket for the speech Marcia had meticulously typed out for him in eighteen-inch font so he could read it easily even if the paper was vibrating from his nerves. He set it down in front of him, smoothing it out with his hands.

The silence felt stifling and he looked up, a sea of expectant faces. Then he looked over to Nathan, who smiled.

"Uh, thanks," he began, gesturing to the plaque. "I, ah, I appreciate it."

The words of the speech that Marcia had written were right there—when he had started the charity, how happy he was that it flourished, how wonderful it was to be here tonight.

He pushed the speech away. For a second, he wondered how it would feel to have Camilla sitting next to him at the dais, smiling at him, sharing the moment. Sharing all the moments.

"I, uh, I started Camp for Kids, and most people probably think I did it for the tax deductions."

There was a laugh from the audience.

"Which are very good."

Polite silence.

His voice was shaky, and he probably wasn't fooling anyone about how nervous he was, but he continued talking anyway.

"I haven't been out to see any of the actual camps or meet the kids, before tonight that is." He looked over to Nathan who was beaming and nodding, making it clear he had met him. "And it's not because I'm so busy or my time is so valuable. It's, uh, sort of for the reason I started the camps in the first place."

He took a deep breath, his heart pounding.

"When I was, uh, little, maybe five or six, some people, I mean my, my family, thought I might have something they called a long, funny name. When I looked it up it meant something they didn't think was very good. They called it Asperger's Syndrome."

The audience was dead silent now, everybody staring at

him, and he rushed to get it out, to say what he had to say.

"It had to do with being different, not what people expected. And it made everybody quite sad to think I might have it. Doctors were involved of course. Diagnoses. About a year or so, it went on and all I remember from that time was how different I really felt. Not good. Not special. *Different.*"

He glanced at Nathan, who had wandered off to Mason's rolls now and wasn't paying attention. Mason looked back at the audience, his voice stronger. "And I didn't like the feeling. Even when all the doctors consulted their guidelines and the results of their tests on me and came back with their pronouncement that I didn't have the horrible thing with the long, funny name, and everybody breathed a sigh of relief, it didn't matter to me. I was still the same kid I was. I was still *different.* And I felt that way my whole life. Different. Not what people expect. I don't feel comfortable in crowds, I don't warm up to people easily, I'm cranky."

The audience laughed.

"That's why I never came before tonight, was afraid to meet people like Nathan here."

That caught the young man's attention, and he stood up and waved. Everybody laughed louder as he grinned and hammed it up, bowing, until the woman next to him said a quiet word and tugged him down.

"Not because he was different," Mason continued. "But because *I* was. And I started Camp for Kids because I wanted a place where they could feel, not different, but *special.*"

The audience clapped and he went on. He had more to say. "A very, ah, extraordinary woman told me once that there are some people who are so evolved they can go on to heaven or Nirvana or whatever…graduate, I guess…"

The audience laughed.

"But sometimes one of those people doesn't go on. Instead, they come back here, to Earth, so we can all learn from them. And *those* people are special. *Special.*"

More than a hundred pairs of eyes watched him, waited for what he was going to say. And he didn't mind it at all. His voice didn't even shake anymore.

"And since she, this, ah, extraordinary woman, was pretty special herself, she knew what she was talking about."

For just a second, he could see Camilla in his mind, and it didn't hurt as much as it usually did. He *had* learned from her. He'd learned he wanted to love someone, he could love someone, and even if they didn't love you back, or couldn't be with you, you were better for it anyway.

And he had learned he loved her. He didn't shy away from it anymore. He knew he did. Whatever that meant or didn't mean to her. And he needed to make sure she knew that.

"So, ah, I'm grateful to have been invited here tonight, by Mrs. Vintilla there." He remembered her name! She smiled and waved, as proud of the mention as Nathan had been. "Because it gave me a chance to remember what Camp for Kids is all about. It's about not letting the fact that we can't give speeches or be what everybody expects us to be or to do s*ome* things," he glanced at the audience where there was a little girl in a wheelchair at a front table, "make us think we're a failure at everything, make us feel anything other than *special*. These kids are special, and I wanted a place where they could feel that."

Abruptly, he went over and sat back down, to his surprise to the accompaniment of thunderous applause. He and

Nathan grinned at each other this time.

The board member returned to the podium, clapping, and said in the microphone, "Now Nathan, let's see if you can top that!"

Nathan popped up, eager to try, and Mason sat back to listen.

At the back of the ballroom, in a chair against the wall on the far left, Camilla held back tears. Marcia slipped into the seat next to her and handed her a tissue. She wiped her eyes.

"That wasn't the speech I wrote for him."

"Did you tell him I was here?"

"Give an old lady some credit," she sniffed. "If he was that nervous already, what do you think knowing you were in the audience would have done to him?"

She laughed.

"Besides, he didn't answer when I called. They must have made him turn off the phone."

Camilla shook her head. "Traitor."

"I know where my loyalties lie. Always! I just think you may be good for him after all."

"I'll try." And she felt very humble about it, too.

A young man was at the podium, talking about the summers he had spent at the camp in upstate New York when he was younger, charming the crowd, reminding Camilla very much of her little brother, especially when it took a few gentle prods from the woman in charge of the microphone to get him to wrap his stories up. But everyone loved it. And

Mason, on the dais, was laughing and smiling with everybody else as he listened, his bow tie untied and his ill-fitting tuxedo jacket on the back of his chair.

"Maybe you'll have more luck with him on the clothes thing," Marcia observed as they watched him, the man she was pretty sure they both loved, in different ways.

She leaned over to the older woman and said, "Mason might not have lucked out on his biological mother, but he did pretty well with you."

The woman reddened, and she handed her the tissue. "And his sperm donor must have really been something," she added, and Marcia laughed.

There were a few more speeches and then the guests were eating desert, drinking cappuccino and starting to file out. Despite that she and Marcia were both considerably underdressed, nobody gave them a second look as they threaded their way through to the dais.

At the last second, Marcia touched her shoulder. "You two need to talk alone. I'll see him tomorrow. Tell him I was proud of him."

"I will." Camilla smiled. "Thanks for the ticket to get me in, and the talk and everything."

"No problem." She headed back out into the crowd as Camilla went on ahead. Deep in conversation, Mason didn't notice as she approached.

The reference to her in his speech—extraordinary, *special,* exactly how she thought about him in fact—had floored her. As much as she wanted to see him, talk to him, suddenly she felt almost shy.

He stopped mid-sentence to see her in front of him. His mouth dropped open, and it took him a second to recover.

The others forged on ahead, filling in the conversational gap as Mason stared at Camilla.

"And so I said to Jennifer that I could too so add in my head and then I—"

"Time to get going, Nathan," the woman who was the master of ceremonies said. "I promised your mother I'd have you home by ten. You, too, Sue. We have to go."

"Oh!"

"Say good-bye to Mr. Talbot."

"Mason," the young man corrected, and Mason turned back to him, smiling.

"That's right." He pulled out a card from his jacket pocket and handed it to him. "Now you give me a call. I'll arrange for a tour of my office, and maybe we could go to lunch."

With vigorous handshakes, the man assured him he would be looking forward to it and then Camilla had Mason to herself.

"He's going to be taking you up on that, you know," she said.

"I'm counting on it."

"Marcia wanted you to know she's proud of you, although she mentioned you didn't use the speech she wrote."

"But I liked the feel of it in my pocket while I was waiting." He gestured to the seats. "Do you want to sit down?"

"Not really. I was hoping maybe I could see that four-story townhouse of yours."

He smiled. "Really? I mean, yes, sure." He glanced around. "Marcia usually arranges a car and calls me with the number."

She put a hand on his arm. "Don't worry. I know how to

catch a cab. Or we could even take the subway."

At his look of horror, she laughed. "Well, maybe you've confronted enough of your fears tonight. We'll save that one for another time."

He took her hands and just that touch felt so right after so long. He swallowed. "I'm not going to have to confront my biggest fear, am I?"

"What's that?" she whispered.

"Not being...*with* you. However you want."

She shook her head. "I've missed you."

He brought her hands to his lips, and she felt sparks at his reverent kiss. "I *ached* for you."

"Yes, and that's part of what I wanted us to prove, to each other and to ourselves."

"That I'm crazy about you?"

"That we're crazy about each other. Although I have to admit I was worried you'd forget about me, like a baby who has his rattle taken away and maybe cries at first but actually thinks the rattle doesn't exist after that and forgets all about it when another toy comes along."

"I'm going to remember to be insulted on both our behalves for that comparison. As soon as I get over being so happy to see my rattle again."

She laughed and he kissed her nose.

"And also, I've made some big changes."

"What? Anything." He pulled her into his arms. "I've never been to Michigan, but I'm sure it's fine, quite nice probably."

"Baby steps," she warned him.

"Anything for my rattle," he teased. "No, really, if you want to go back to Michigan, I'll go with you, if you'll let me."

"No, I won't plunge you back into the lion's den just yet."

"I'll be better—"

"Shhh." She held a finger to his lips, looking into those sincere eyes. God, she loved him! Even if she had to take some time to say it. Had to say it carefully. "You'll fit in just fine with my family. I never should have doubted it. I love *different*. It's an Anderson family trait. And after what you said up here just now, well, my parents couldn't have hand-picked a better man for me if they'd done it themselves."

He tightened his hold on her. "Yes, but how do we convince them of that?"

"They'll love you. Joey already does. He keeps asking me when I'm going to bring you around again, if you can believe it."

"I'd like that."

"And thank you for the donation."

"What donation?" He kept his face straight, but thinned his lips at the effort.

"*And* I like that you're a bad liar."

He laughed. "You're welcome in that case."

She brushed the hair out of his eyes, lingering on the soft, springy curls. "My career was the other thing I wanted to figure out and I have. I've entered an MFA program."

"A what?"

"Masters of Fine Arts, in writing. At a small college fifty minutes out of Manhattan. I start there in the fall, and you know the best thing?"

"You're only fifty minutes out of Manhattan?"

"Well, that and not only is the program fully funded—because they know anybody who wants to be a writer is a dreamer anyway and has no money." She wrapped her arms around his neck. "But also my law school student loans will be deferred for the time I'm in school. A grace period!"

"That's great." He kissed her and every plan she ever had went out of her head...again! But this time she could stick to her plans and give them the time they needed to explore, each other and life...together.

"And when I get out," she said. "Who knows? Maybe I'll spend hours writing the great American novel with you beside me spending hours refining that thing-a-ma-jiggy your company produces. But I'm not planning that far ahead. Not this time. I'm, ah, enjoying the ride."

"With me?" he whispered.

"Absolutely with you. Now let's go check out that townhouse. I'll flag the cab."

"Hang on." He reached into his pocket. "Turn around."

When he clasped her pearls around her neck, his thumb slipped under the strand to caress her collarbone and she melted. He said, low, "I've been carrying these around all this time we've been apart, like somehow they'd magically bring you back to me."

She smiled. "You brought me back to you. You are *special*. And I'm not going anywhere this time."

Hand in hand, they caught a cab.

## The End

# Acknowledgments

Much thanks to the very professional team at Entangled for all their help and encouragement.

# About the Author

Angela Claire, like most writers, grew up loving to read, which led to a degree in English literature, which in turn led to unemployment. Not having been born to wealth, Angela developed a more practical plan for eating and paying her rent—hence the dreaded and expected descent into law school and inevitable career as a lawyer. Once she paid off her pesky yet massive student loans, Angela saved for an escape from the law profession one day. Now a multi-published author, she does what she loves, but with a little less leeway on the eating and paying rent thing.

Visit her online at www.angelaclaireromance.com